THE BILLIONAIRE COWBOY TAKES A WIFE

Wives for the Western Billionaires 1

Paige Cameron

EVERLASTING CLASSIC

Siren Publishing, Inc.
www.SirenPublishing.com

A SIREN PUBLISHING BOOK
IMPRINT: Everlasting Classic

THE BILLIONAIRE COWBOY TAKES A WIFE
Copyright © 2011 by Paige Cameron

ISBN-10: 1-61034-688-2
ISBN-13: 978-1-61034-688-7

First Printing: June 2011

Cover design by *Les Byerley*
All art and logo copyright © 2011 by Siren Publishing, Inc.

Printed in the U.S.A.

PUBLISHER
Siren Publishing, Inc.
www.SirenPublishing.com

DEDICATION

To all the best friends out there, who make our lives a little easier and a lot more fun. You know who you are.

THE BILLIONAIRE COWBOY TAKES A WIFE

Wives for the Western Billionaires 1

PAIGE CAMERON
Copyright © 2011

Chapter One

Jackson Stone sat back and enjoyed watching Samantha Riley pace across his home office. Her T-shirt and tight jeans gave him a good view of her curves and sweet derriere. Sunlight from two large windows sparkled over her golden hair and lit up her sherry-colored eyes. He only half-listened to her angry mumblings regarding her grandfather.

Suddenly, she stopped and leaned over his desk. She directed her glare at him.

"Marry me."

"What?" Jackson leaned further back in his chair.

"Marry me. It will tickle Gramps, and our two ranches will connect as one. Although," she took a breath and added, "I still plan on managing mine."

"Sit, slow down, and start over. I must have missed something important in all your rantings."

Her sherry-colored eyes flashed. "You weren't listening. Gramps has threatened to disinherit me if I don't marry and give him a grandchild." She swung away and began to pace again. "I don't care about the inheritance, except for the Diamond R Ranch. If my cousin,

Floyd, gets it, he'll sell the ranch. Gramps knows this. He can't be serious."

"And yet you believe it enough to propose to me?"

She flopped into the chair across from him. "Well, what else can I do? You and I have been friends since I moved here. We'd do all right as a couple. *I think*."

"What happened to Mr. Perfect?"

A flush crossed her face. "We weren't suited." She glanced toward the windows. "He said I was too independent, outspoken, and a number of other such adjectives."

His laugh brought a frown his way. "Sorry. But you know he's right."

"Maybe," she admitted reluctantly. "Will you?"

"Will I what?"

"Don't be dense. Will you marry me?"

Jackson studied her face. He remembered when she came to live at the Diamond R Ranch after her parents' death in an auto accident. The ten-year-old, gangly girl followed her grandfather around constantly and in the process met Jackson, who was fourteen. They became good friends.

He'd taught her to ride and shoot a gun. On hot summer days they went swimming at an old water hole on his ranch. His parents loved her.

Over the years she'd occasionally been an annoyance, teasing him about his dates, and once tried to run a girl off that she didn't like. Of course, he'd retaliated by dunking her in a mud hole. He smiled in remembrance of her fury.

"Jackson, you're not listening to me." Her voice snapped him back to the present. "Will you help me or not?"

"Helping you with a project at school or on the ranch is a little different than going into a marriage."

"I know that. Think about it and come to dinner tonight. You can ask Gramps about his ultimatum. He'll tell you."

"All right, I don't mind enjoying one of Maria's good meals, but I'm not promising anything."

"Right. Dinner's at six." She waved and disappeared as quickly as she'd come.

He went to the window and watched her swing up onto Princess, her favorite mare. She had a good seat. Without looking back, she galloped across the field toward home.

Jackson went to his side bar. He reached for a crystal glass, filled it with ice, and poured bourbon in. A little early for a drink, but he needed one. His body throbbed with desire, and his cock was rock hard. He'd fought to not show his emotions.

Never did he expect to have what he wanted most tossed into his lap. He'd hidden his real feelings from her for over ten years. Even now, he could recall the first time a flash of desire for her had coursed through him.

She'd been eighteen and just out of high school heading for college. He'd just returned from his college graduation. He hid the new feelings, thinking to wait until she had time to get her own college degree. He'd kept in touch. He still waited. She'd never seen him as any more than a friend.

She'd shared with him her funny tales of love and love lost, not realizing the sense of relief that washed over him each time her relationships ended. Determined to win her, he'd asked her out on a date. It'd been about seven years ago. She'd laughed.

"We can't date, Jackson. We like each other too much, and it might ruin our friendship."

Resigning himself to finding someone else, he'd dated a number of beautiful, talented women, but none had Samantha's fire, none touched him inside.

He took a long swallow of bourbon. The liquid burned his throat and warmed his belly. Did he dare take her as his wife? He certainly wouldn't agree to a platonic relationship. The men she'd dated and tossed aside were right. She was all the things she mentioned—

independent, headstrong, with too much sass in her talk. He smiled and savored another swallow of his drink. But unlike them, he wasn't afraid of the challenge she represented, and her timing was perfect. He had almost all the arrangements made to turn over his conglomerate of businesses to someone else. He just hadn't made the final decision of who he'd choose, and no one, not even Samantha, could know his plans yet.

He glanced at his clock. There was a lot of work to get done before dinner. He looked forward to the challenges he'd meet tonight. There were no doubts in his mind that she'd have second thoughts. He'd have to stay one step ahead of her.

* * * *

Samantha pulled up at the barn and dismounted, handing her reins to one of the ranch hands.

"Your grandpa said to tell you he wants to see you in his study," the man said.

She nodded and strode across the dusty ground toward the house. The enormity of what she'd done hadn't hit her until she was riding home. She'd actually asked Jackson to marry her. Last night's argument and her lack of sleep must have knocked her senseless.

Sure, Jackson was her best male friend, but she'd not thought of him in a romantic way since she was sixteen and had a secret crush on him. Why she hadn't pursued a relationship, she wasn't sure.

He was handsome and apparently a successful businessman. She'd never really asked much about his work outside of his ranch. She was certain women found him attractive. He'd had a number of girlfriends in high school. But, she'd always sensed strength in him that wouldn't bend or waiver, and while that might be a good characteristic in a friend, she wasn't sure she wanted it in a husband.

She admitted she was independent, sassy, and stubborn. She didn't plan to change. No, she had made a mistake. A marriage between them could never work. Two strong-willed people like Jackson and her would butt heads. A marriage between them would be a disaster.

The problem was how to take her offer back. If Gramps got wind of it, he'd hold her to her words.

Stepping onto the wide porch, she took off her hat. The temperature dropped several degrees in the shade. The old homestead had been built a hundred years ago, and she loved the history and feeling of love captured inside the walls. Here she felt safe and loved.

She let the screen door slam behind her. "I'm home, Gramps."

A tall, lean, white-haired man stepped into the hall. "I know when the door slams, it's you," he grumbled.

"Grumble, grumble, don't you love me anymore, Gramps?" Her smile belied her question.

"Don't need to ask. You know the answer. Doesn't mean I'm recalling what I said last night. It's time a man took control of you and this ranch. I'm getting too old, and I want a great grandson or granddaughter to bounce on my knee before I die."

"Did the doctor tell you your end is near?" she teased, knowing he might be old, but Gramps was a long way from spending his time in a rocker.

"Don't get smart. You've had plenty of time to find a man on your own. I've been patient, and now I'm taking over."

Samantha strolled toward the kitchen door. "Is Maria here yet?"

"Course she is. You're just trying to change the subject. It's fine with me. You have six weeks to show me an engagement ring before I change my will." With those words, he strode out the door and headed to his car.

Opening the kitchen door, she saw Maria rolling out a pie crust. "Smells good in here, Maria. What's for dinner?"

Maria turned toward her. "It's not lunch yet. Why are you interested in dinner?"

"We're having company. Jackson will be joining us."

Maria grinned. "He's not company, more like family. I'm baking an apple pie. That's his favorite. I'll set an extra plate."

"Thanks." Samantha poured herself a cup of coffee and grabbed a biscuit from a platter. "If anyone's looking for me, I've gone for a walk."

"Hiding from your grandfather won't solve your problems."

"Do you know what he wants me to do?"

Maria nodded. "I didn't eavesdrop. Anyone inside the house couldn't avoid hearing yesterday's discussion."

"He can't be serious," Samantha repeated for at least the tenth time.

"He is, and I think he's right."

Samantha's mouth dropped open. "How can you agree with his ridiculous demand?"

"He wants what's best for you."

"Yeah," Samantha snorted and went out the side door. A line of trees created a shady area behind the house, and she walked to the most distant one and sat with her back against the rough bark.

Not since she'd first come to live with her grandparents had she felt so unsettled. Three years ago her grandmother died. After a year of private grieving, Gramps turned his attention back to work, and now her.

Samantha pulled her cell phone out of her pocket and speed dialed her best girlfriend, Janice. The phone rang four times before the familiar answering machine picked up. Samantha snapped her phone shut and stared across the open fields at the cattle and horses gazing in nearby pastures.

She could not lose the ranch. The ranch had been the one constant in her life. She had lost too much of her family to death. She couldn't control the circumstances that took them from her. But, the land and the work she'd been sure she'd have forever. She studied agriculture, and after getting her degree, she'd come home expecting to stay. In her mind whoever married her would want to live on the ranch and help her.

Well, maybe her dreams had been a little unrealistic. That's why she'd thought of Jackson this morning. He had other businesses, but since his parents sold him the ranch, retired, and went traveling, Jackson had come home more often. Married, she'd be a help by being here all the time and taking care of both places.

He'll want a real marriage. The thought of Jackson and her in bed sent heat rushing through her veins. His six-foot-three-inch frame was lean and hard. Add golden brown hair, eyes the color of the summer sky, a dimple in his left cheek, and a girl could melt into a puddle at his feet. He exuded raw masculinity. Before today, she'd never allowed herself to consider him in a romantic way. She wasn't sure why.

She hated to admit it, but he was stronger than her, and not just physically. Her demands and arguments had always rolled off his broad shoulders. She'd been the one to apologize because she didn't want to lose his friendship. Being married to him, she might lose herself. It was too much of a risk.

She'd explain tonight that she'd been overly emotional and sprouted off without thinking. He didn't want to marry her, not really. He hadn't even accepted her offer yet. She had nothing to worry about. They'd both laugh about her silly proposal and settle back into their comfortable friendship.

That didn't solve her problem though. Where could she find the right man? He had to love the country, want to live at the ranch, and not mind her control issues. *All right*, she admitted, *I do like to be in control.*

Her cell rang. "Hello," Samantha answered.

"I've thought about your offer. I accept." His deep, husky voice sent shivers through her.

"Don't you want to talk with Gramps first?"

"Sure. Tonight I'll ask his permission to marry you. He's old-fashioned, and I respect him. He'll expect the question."

"We need to talk first."

"Is there a problem?"

She heard the smile in his voice. "I may have been rash in trying to force you to my way of thinking."

"No problem. I think you're right. We'll deal well with each other, and my folks and your grandfather will be overjoyed."

Darn, what could she say now? If he asked Gramps to marry her, the deal was sealed and stamped. For once, she admitted her rashness had gotten her into a corner.

"We'll talk tonight, before you see Gramps."

"See you at six."

She snapped her phone shut, realizing he had not agreed with her last demand. This situation was swirling out of control, and she had no one to blame but herself.

* * * *

Samantha paced across her bedroom. Outside her window the sun set with colors of gold and red painting the sky. She glanced at her watch, five forty-five. Jackson had been due at six, but she'd heard him arrive five minutes ago. He'd greeted Gramps while she stood nearby, unseen. When the study door snapped closed, she tiptoed back to her room.

She'd hoped to have a few words with Jackson first. Too late now. This was one time her impetuous behavior had gotten her into a situation where she saw no way out.

"Sam." Maria called out her pet name and then knocked on the door. "Your grandfather wants you to join him and Jackson in the study."

Samantha slid her hands over the short, champagne-colored dress she wore. She'd left her hair hanging loose. She opened the door.

"Tell Gramps I'm not quite ready."

"You look beautiful," Maria said.

That was the problem. "This is too dressy. I don't know what I was thinking."

Maria shook her head. "I never thought of you as a coward." She took Samantha's hand. "Come on, you know Mr. Riley will get annoyed if you hold up dinner."

Reluctantly, Samantha followed her. The study door stood slightly ajar. She heard male voices talking quietly on the other side.

Samantha pushed the door open. Both Jackson and Gramps stood at her entrance.

"Samantha, why didn't you tell me the good news earlier today?" Smiling broadly, Gramps walked around his desk, his arms outstretched. She walked into his hug. His fragrance of Old Spice with a hint of his cigar smoke surrounded her. An unexpected rush of love and sadness had her blinking her eyes.

Gramps stepped back still holding onto her shoulders. "You've made me very happy." He glanced across at Jackson. "Jackson's already almost like a son to me. He'll keep you and the ranch safe."

For the first time since she'd entered the room, Samantha looked at her prospective husband. Standing quietly to the side, he watched the two of them intently. His blue eyes had darkened, and his expression gave away none of his feelings. When his eyes connected with hers, a slow smile crossed his face. He took a leisurely survey of her from her head to her toes peeking out of gold sandals. A rush of heat went straight to her face.

"Darling." He strolled toward her. Then he leaned down, brushing her lips with his. A shiver ran across her shoulders and down her spine. "I know we talked about waiting to tell your grandfather. But I had to ask for his permission to marry you before we fly to Houston tomorrow to choose an engagement ring."

"Tomorrow? We're herding the cattle from the west range. I can't possibly go until later this week."

"Nonsense," Gramps said. "This is much more important. I have plenty of help."

"I'll send two of my men over, just in case they're needed," Jackson said.

"Fine. See, Samantha, you have nothing to worry about except your wedding." Gramps nodded at her. "You'll need to get used to the men doing the hard work. I'm sure Jackson has other plans for his wife."

Jackson had a devilish grin on his face. Samantha frowned at him. She'd better set this matter straight right now.

"My future husband has agreed I can run the ranches while he travels with his business. That will work best for both of us."

Gramps frowned at her and Jackson. "What foolishness is this? Jackson, did you agree to this?"

"It's not decided yet, Sir."

"We did decide," Samantha snapped.

"We'll talk later, darling."

"Don't darling me." Samantha began to pace around the room.

"You'll have your hands full, son. Still, few people know her better than you."

"We'll do fine, Mr. Riley."

"I expect you will. Too bad my wife didn't live to see this happy day. She was very fond of you. Enough discussion for now. We'd better head to the dining room. There's no need to let Maria's good food get cold." Gramps slapped Jackson on the shoulder. "This good news has given me an appetite."

They both turned to let Samantha lead the way. Frowning at both men, she stomped down the hall. Just wait until she got Jackson alone. She'd rip him a good one.

Chapter Two

Dinner went by quickly. Gramps and Jackson discussed ranching issues. Samantha would have usually jumped into the conversation, but she was too flustered and instead picked at her food.

"Are you all right?" Gramps asked, turning his attention to her.

"I'm not hungry."

Gramps grinned at Jackson. "Too much excitement." Then they continued talking.

Samantha looked across the table and watched Jackson's fleeting expressions as he listened to Gramps. The old chandelier, made of cow horns, hung directly over the dining room table, and the light brought out the gold in Jackson's hair.

He used his strong, capable hands to describe something to Gramps. Samantha found herself imagining him touching her, sliding his fingers along her neck to her breasts. She blinked. What was wrong with her? She never fantasized about a man making love to her. The talking had stopped. Both men stared at her.

Gramps reached across and touched her forehead. "You're flushed and you feel hot. I hope you're not getting sick."

"I'm fine, Gramps, really, but it is warm in here. If you two will excuse me, I'll step outside on the porch to cool off."

Jackson shoved back his chair. "I'm finished. I'll join you." A teasing light shone in his eyes.

Surely he had no idea of her thoughts. She'd die of embarrassment. He pulled her chair back and followed her out the front door. At least now she'd have a chance to talk with him. Renewed anger at how he'd rushed things tonight began to build inside her. She walked to the far corner where they had more privacy. Jackson followed and stopped right behind her.

Whirling around, she confronted him. "Why didn't you wait? I told you I'd just been my emotional self and said things I didn't mean."

"The reality is you need a husband, and I want a wife. Your grandfather is pleased. We're good friends. What can be wrong with the outcome?"

"That's just the trouble. We are friends. I can't imagine us being more."

"Oh, I believe you can and did back there in the dining room."

"How ridiculous. I don't know what you're talking about."

"Well, if your only concern about us is as a couple, let me put your mind to rest." His big hands cupped her face. Startled, she gasped and stared up at him as he slowly lowered his head.

His mouth softly brushed across her eyelashes, whispered along her cheek, before settling on her lips. His tongue moved along her tightly closed mouth until she opened for him. He pulled her closer into his warm embrace as his tongue tangled with hers then moved along the edge of her teeth.

Her tingling breasts were tight against his firm chest. With one arm, he anchored her lower body against his hard arousal. She went weak, and heat flashed over her. Without thought, her arms went around his neck, and she moaned. Abruptly, he dropped his arms and stepped back. She swayed. He reached out to steady her.

"See. You don't need to have any concerns about us."

Samantha took a deep breath, giving herself time to pull her thoughts together. "This proves nothing. I've responded to a few of the men I've dated, but the very few who I've been intimate with have left me questioning what all the fuss is about. Sex is definitely overrated."

Jackson's laugh startled her. "I'm serious, Jackson. You don't want to be married to a cold woman." She found her cheeks heating again. Although they'd been close friends, she and Jackson had never discussed sex.

Jackson pulled her back into his arms, but more of a comforting hold this time. His hand ran through her hair. "Don't worry. I'd never describe you as cold. Trust me to take care of any doubts you may have."

She pulled away. Part of her had wanted to stay enclosed in his arms, but she mustn't. She would not allow him to make her weak. "This is all becoming much more than I'd planned."

He moved to her side and stared out in the distance. "And your plan was what?"

"That we'd have a business deal, a sensible marriage."

Turning to face her, his finger tipped her face up. "I will not agree to anything less than a committed marriage with, hopefully, children. Do you want to tell your grandfather the engagement is off, or shall we leave it that if you are at the airfield at seven tomorrow, you are agreeing to my terms?"

His eyes were hard and his expression stony. She knew he meant what he said. At least he'd given her tonight to think and to talk with Gramps once more.

"If I'm at the airport, then I've agreed with your terms."

She walked to the front door and went inside.

* * * *

Jackson let out his breath. He'd put her in a corner, which had never been wise, but he had no intention of agreeing to a business marriage. At least not with Samantha. When she'd walked into the study earlier, all his blood left his head and went straight to his cock. Thankfully, Samantha and Gramps didn't look at him until he had better control of himself.

He wanted her with a deep passion. He wanted to breathe in her scent, slide his hands over her golden, tanned skin, kiss those luscious breasts, and bury himself deep inside her. But he'd risked it all on his ultimatum. Knowing Samantha, she was inside now trying to convince her grandfather to change his mind about his demand she marry.

Jackson strode across the porch and out over the lawn to his truck. Tonight, he rolled down the windows, preferring the cool night air to the air-conditioning. As he drove toward his ranch, he breathed deeply and the familiar fragrances of cattle, soil, and the sweetness of the wildflowers mingled together. This was the one place on earth that was home. His fancy townhouse in Houston and the oceanfront home in Florida were places where he resided temporarily. Like the ranch, Samantha was home for him, too. He planned on marrying her, one way or the other.

* * * *

Samantha found Gramps resting in his favorite chair. "Gramps, can we talk?"

"Certainly, but first let Maria know we'll have coffee and dessert. Did Jackson leave?"

"Yes. I'll go tell Maria." She hurried to the kitchen where Maria had just finished cleaning up. "Gramps is ready for dessert."

Maria smiled and walked over, cupping Samantha's face in her hands. She bent forward and kissed her forehead. "Congratulations. You've made Mr. Riley very happy. Jackson will be an excellent husband for you."

"How can you be sure? We've always been just friends."

Maria patted her cheek and chuckled. "The love has been just underneath. I'm glad you both finally realized it. What beautiful babies you'll make."

"Maria, we aren't even married yet."

"I doubt Jackson will let you have a long engagement. I expect he's been ready for a family for some time."

Samantha just stared at her. Maria had been their cook, housekeeper, and almost like a nanny to her. Maria's words stunned her.

"Here, take in the coffee. I'll bring the apple pie."

"We only need two servings. Jackson left."

"What? He's going to regret leaving early when I tell him he missed my pie. Well, you can take him some tomorrow."

Rather than say any more, Samantha took the coffee tray and went back to Gramps. She was in a pickle of a fix. Gramps wouldn't change his mind about his will, and she'd upset him and Maria if she called off the engagement.

She'd call Janice. With her level head and realistic way of looking at situations, she was the best person to advise her. As soon as they had dessert, she'd excuse herself and call Janice from the privacy of her bedroom.

Samantha found something unimportant to talk with Gramps about, and as soon as they finished dessert, she excused herself.

"It's best you get to bed early," Gramps said. "Jackson said you'd be flying out at seven. You've made me happy and proud. Have fun tomorrow finding the perfect ring."

"I will," she lied. "See you after I return." Samantha waved and walked briskly down the hall and upstairs to her room. She grabbed her cell phone and snuggled into the chair by her window. With all the lights out, except for a nightlight, hundreds of stars twinkled in the darkness.

Hitting the familiar number for Janice, she leaned back in the chair listening to the dial tone. Hopefully, she'd be home.

"Hello."

"Janice, I'm so glad you didn't go out tonight."

"Sam? I noticed you'd called earlier. I planned to return the call, but it's been a hectic day. I just got home."

"Got time to talk?"

"Sure, I've just poured myself a glass of wine. I'm all ears."

"I'm engaged."

"What? To whom? You never hinted you were even close to anyone."

Samantha told her about Gramps' demand, and her sudden decision to propose to Jackson.

"Whoa, girl, when you do it, you do it big. You've always said you two didn't feel that way about each other."

"We don't. At least I don't. I'm not sure about Jackson anymore. I tried to retract my offer, but Jackson accepted anyway and told Gramps about our engagement."

"I see. One of your impetuous ideas backfired on you. Still, Jackson is a very desirable man. There are plenty of women here in Houston that would do anything to marry him. So what's the problem?"

"I want a businesslike marriage. I'd even thought of having you draw up a contract for us." Janice's laughter on the other end stopped her.

"A business marriage with Jackson? Honey, have you lost your mind?"

"This is serious, Janice. I need your advice."

"Oh no, Sam. I'm not getting into the middle of this. That's how people lose friends."

"You're not going to help me?"

"Nope. Sleep on it. Come into town and have lunch soon."

"We're picking out a ring tomorrow."

Janice went into peals of laughter again. "Go with it friend. Look at the man. Don't be crazy, grab him. Got to go, love you."

Samantha stared at the phone. Everyone had deserted her. She'd never sleep. She'd sit right here and find a way out of this mess by morning.

Chapter Three

Jackson didn't comment when she arrived at the airport, which was just as well. She'd barely slept and had missed her coffee. He helped her into the helicopter and put on her headset for her.

"This is Fred. He's a good pilot, so try to relax. I remember flying isn't your favorite thing to do," Jackson said, giving her one of those smiles that always made her feel better. He settled back in the seat beside her as the blades began to turn.

Samantha tried to relax as the big bird took off, but when the pilot banked the helicopter to the left, she found herself grabbing Jackson's leg. She snatched her hand back. "Sorry."

"Don't be." He enclosed her hand in his and put their hands back on his leg. The temperature around them rose at least ten degrees.

Trying to ignore him, Samantha glanced out the window. Down below, a carpet of bluebells spread across the wide prairie. If not for her current problems, she'd enjoy the beautiful sight. But, she found the man beside her impossible to ignore. Today he'd dressed as a successful business man—dark brown suit, cream-colored vest, a tie colored in shades of brown and cream. He looked good enough to eat. Now where did that come from? What was happening to her? This was Jackson, *her friend.*

She was determined to quit thinking about him, but her body was attuned to his every move. When his leg brushed against her, her skin prickled. His scent tantalized her nose. Samantha forced herself to concentrate on the sights below and the beautiful blue sky around her. She might as well relax. The flight usually took close to two hours.

When the pilot banked to head more directly toward Houston,

Samantha leaned into Jackson. His arms wrapped around her.

"Are you all right?"

"My stomach doesn't like sudden moves."

"Put your arms around me and hang on. We'll be there soon."

His heart thumped under her ear. Strong arms held her close, and his musky, masculine scent filled her head when she took a deep breath. She wrapped her arms around his firm body. Lean and hard, he didn't have an ounce of fat on him. He stroked her hair as her body began to relax against his warmth. She'd barely dozed off when she heard his voice.

"Wake up, sleeping beauty." Jackson brushed a kiss across the top of her head.

Samantha blinked her eyes. "I wasn't asleep."

"You snored, darlin'. You were definitely asleep for a few moments."

She straightened and then smoothed her blouse and skirt. "Sorry."

"No problem. You can sleep on my body anytime." He laughed when the heat rushed to her face.

Before he could say anything else, someone opened the door. "Where are we?" Samantha looked around. They'd landed on the top of a very tall building, clustered in the middle of other concrete structures of various heights. Jackson turned to her and removed her headset. "This is my office building. I need to check in." He stepped out, and then took her hand and assisted her out.

The wind swirled around the rooftop. She was glad she'd worn slacks. In the distance, she heard the faint sound of a car horn. His building? She'd known he had a successful business, but to own the whole building, in an obviously busy section of downtown, then he must be doing extremely well.

A man, dressed in a dark suit, walked out of a nearby door. He spoke to Jackson and ushered them inside to a small foyer and then into the waiting elevator.

"Samantha, this is one of my senior associates, Oliver Greenlee.

Oliver, my fiancée, Samantha Riley."

Samantha saw the shock on Mr. Greenlee's face, but he hid it quickly. "Congratulations, Sir and Ms. Riley." He nodded his head and smiled at her.

"Thanks, Oliver. We're going to be shopping part of the day," Jackson said. "Any business that needs my attention before we leave?"

"There's a problem in Singapore."

A slight frown crossed Jackson's face. "We'll talk in my office. Mrs. Haverty can get Sam a cup of coffee while she waits."

The elevator opened to a luxurious lounge with carpet that Samantha's shoes sank into and large leather chairs in a deep gold color. An older woman, short and plump with a wide smile, came around her desk and greeted them. Jackson did a quick introduction and headed for the door marked with his name in gold letters.

"I'll be just a few minutes, Samantha. Mrs. Haverty, will you get her coffee and a roll, if you can find one? My fiancée skipped breakfast."

With those words, he disappeared into his office, followed by Oliver. While Mrs. Haverty went for her coffee, Samantha speed-dialed Janice at her office.

"The law offices of Black, Simmons, and Dedrick," the receptionist announced.

"May I speak to Ms. Dedrick?"

"One minute please."

"Janice Dedrick, may I help you?"

"Yes, help me."

"Ah, I know that voice. You're in town?"

"Waiting for Jackson. He's meeting with *one* of his associates. Did you know he owns this building?"

Janice chuckled. "He owns a lot more than that building. I've always been surprised how you've never inquired about any of his concerns but the ranch."

"And you didn't tell me."

"You didn't seem interested and didn't ask."

"Can we get together for lunch?"

"I thought you were picking out an engagement ring?"

"We are sometime today. I don't intend to sit around too long waiting for him to remember me."

"Check with Jackson. If you're free, how about meeting at our favorite Italian place?"

"Great. Unless I call back, plan on seeing me at noon."

"It's a date." Janice hung up just as Jackson came striding through his door.

"This is going to take longer than I'd thought. I've called my housekeeper, Anna Murphy. She'll be waiting for you at my townhouse. My chauffeur will drive you there."

"Whoa. Housekeeper and chauffeur? What's wrong with me taking a taxi?"

"Why?" Jackson gave her a puzzled look.

"Because I'm not used to all of this." She spread her hands to encompass the lovely room. "I'm a plain cowgirl, remember?"

He ignored her comment. "I have one more surprise. You have an appointment at the spa, downstairs from my condo apartment, to have a massage and facial in an hour."

"I'm meeting Janice for lunch at twelve."

Jackson raised an eyebrow, but the arrival of his secretary stopped him from whatever he planned to say. Mrs. Haverty had a tray with coffee, juice, and toast.

"Thanks, Mrs. Haverty. See that she eats and then have the car brought around front for her." He turned back to Samantha. "We're going to a fancy party tonight. If you didn't bring a gown with you, go shopping and put it on my card." He went to hand her his credit card.

Samantha backed away. "We aren't married yet. I can buy my own clothes." She found herself frowning at his back and listening to his laugh as he strode quickly into his office and closed the door.

The coffee and food did make her feel more like herself. Mrs. Haverty very efficiently had her in the car and headed to Jackson's townhouse in no time. The car slowed and parked in front of another impressive, tall building. The front double doors had elaborate etching on the glass panels. Her chauffeur opened the car door, and she stepped out. Glancing at her watch, she saw it had only taken fifteen minutes to get here.

The doorman greeted her by name and opened the doors to the lobby. Mrs. Haverty must have called ahead. Samantha's head spun with all this attention. She'd never suspected Jackson had such prominence in the business world. She had always been single-minded concerning ranching and living in the country. Even if she did begin to have feelings for Jackson, she doubted she'd ever get used to or like living in the city.

Large vases of mixed flowers and some of orchids were scattered around the palatial lobby, sending a sweet fragrance into the air. The doorman directed her to a separate elevator.

"This one goes straight to the penthouse. Mrs. Murphy is expecting you."

"Thank you..." She glanced at his name tag. "Harold."

She stepped into the mirrored elevator, and it shot smoothly to the top, leaving her stomach behind. She really didn't like all these high buildings. The doors slid open to a large foyer. Highly polished dark wood covered the walls. Another vase filled with long-stemmed red roses sat on a small table by the double doors, which stood open. A tall, broad-shouldered woman with gray hair and friendly brown eyes stood at the entrance, smiling at her.

"You must be Miss Riley. Come in. Mrs. Haverty called ahead to tell me to expect you." She opened the door wider, and Samantha moved inside. The living room looked like something out of one of the house and garden magazines. A soft blend of yellows and blues welcomed her. To the left, a long line of patio doors stood open to a wide balcony.

"Why don't you look around while I get you some tea?" Mrs. Murphy looked at her watch. "You have about a half hour before your massage appointment." She walked briskly along a hallway and turned right.

Samantha followed her and saw a gleaming white kitchen. She continued to stroll along the hall, noticing a study on the left and two bedrooms on the right. At the end were another set of double doors. This must be the master bedroom. Her hand hesitated on the door knob, but curiosity got the better of her.

The doors opened into a cozy sitting room. One wall lined with books, and on the other side a large television. A single door on the left led into the enormous bedroom. Shades of gray and blue color were integrated into the walls, the curtains, and the bedspread, giving a soothing ambiance.

Drapes covered the right wall. When she pushed a round, silver button located right beside them, they slid back, exposing another set of doors which opened to a smaller balcony. From here, a wide, expansive view of the city spread out before her. She stepped outside. Wind blew her hair wildly around her. Cautiously, she moved forward. It really was a wonderful panoramic view.

"Your tea, Miss Riley." Anna had stepped out behind her. "Perhaps you'd like to sit here for a few minutes." She motioned to a chair by a small table. "Jackson likes to start his morning reading his paper out here." She smiled, in a motherly fashion, each time she spoke of Jackson.

"No. I'll be right back inside."

"Take your time."

Samantha started to follow her when she saw another door on the other side of the room. She walked across the deep, plush carpet and pushed the door open, exposing a luxurious bath. The tile was a dark green and white. In one corner was a large shower with mirrors all around and several showerheads set at different angles. Across the room, a long vanity held two sinks and to the right, opposite the shower, was a huge, sunken, jetted tub. It was really quite decadent and nothing she would have expected of Jackson. She'd begun to wonder if she knew him at all.

She glanced at her watch. She barely had time to drink her tea and get downstairs to the spa. Hurriedly, she retraced her steps to the lounge area.

* * * *

Samantha stepped out of the black limousine in front of the small Italian restaurant she and Janice had found several years ago. It was tucked away on the outskirts of town. Several people glanced at her and the shiny, long car. Tempting smells of pizza and other Italian delights drifted out to the street. Taking off her sunglasses, she strolled into the dining room searching for her friend. She saw Janice wave from their favorite corner booth and headed her way.

"You look great," Janice said.

"I feel pretty great. I just had a massage and facial which included new makeup for my face."

"Whoever did the job knew their business. The right colors with a light touch. But you've never cared for anything but powder and a light blush."

"Jackson arranged it. Well, I didn't know about the makeup part, but we're going to a party. I guess he didn't want me embarrassing him as the country cousin, so to speak."

"I doubt that. You always look beautiful. Still, the light colors do bring out your eyes."

"Enough, please. Tell me how I'm going to get out of this mess. He's apparently terribly rich. I'll never fit in."

The waiter stepped up to their table. "Would you ladies like to order?" They ordered their favorite, a supreme, thick-crust pizza and side salad. Once he left, Samantha stared at her friend, trying to get

Janice to give her an answer to the predicament she'd gotten herself into.

"He is very rich and well-respected. I'm not sure if you realize the busy social life he has in town. Women flock to him."

"Has he ever had a serious relationship?"

Janice nodded. "Several over the years, one woman I thought for sure he'd marry, but he took over his parents' ranch about that time, and soon after they split."

"I remember. He brought her to the ranch once. Pretty, blonde, tiny, hung on his every word," Samantha said.

"That would be her. I believe since you saw her, you must have seen Jackson and her together. Seeing her and you side by side must have made Jackson realize he still cared for you."

"You think he's cared for me, a long time?"

"I do. And I don't think there's any way he'll let you out of this deal you made."

Samantha's head spun with all the surprises she'd discovered today. Jackson may have been her friend, but his world encompassed so much more than she'd expected. She'd never fit in. After the party tonight, he'd see how unprepared she was to be the type of wife he needed.

Their steaming hot pizza and small salads were placed on their table, stopping any further conversation while they savored the delicious food. Samantha took a last bite of her pizza and sat back.

"How's your business?" she asked Janice.

"Good. Actually, Jackson sends work my way quite often."

"Really?"

"Don't be so surprised. I'm a good corporate lawyer. And speaking of Jackson, don't look now, but he's headed our way."

Samantha glanced around and saw him weaving his way around the crowded room in their direction. In a few long strides, he arrived at their table.

"Ladies, I hope I'm not interrupting. How are you, Janice?"

"Busy. I'm glad to see you, but I've got to run. You can have my seat."

"No, Janice, please stay." Samantha put out her hand.

"Wish I could. Call me later." She turned and walked briskly off.

Jackson sat and reached across, taking Samantha's hand. "Hope I didn't break up your visit. I got finished early and thought I'd grab a bite to eat with you before our appointment."

Samantha didn't reply as the waiter had come to the table to take his order. After deciding on a salad and a small pizza, he glanced across at her.

"I'm having a glass of merlot. Do you want something besides that tea?" He motioned to her glass. "Be daring and join me in a glass of wine."

Against her will, she smiled. "All right, I'll have a glass of Riesling." The waiter nodded and hurried off.

"Did you and Janice have a nice visit?"

"It was too short. But, I'm glad you came. We need to talk."

Again, he enclosed his fingers around her hand. "Talk."

She didn't want to admit she found it difficult to think clearly when he was rubbing his thumb across her palm. Those new jittery feelings swept over her at his touch. She wet her dry lips.

"You never told me you were rich and owned buildings and lived in a place straight out of a magazine. You have a chauffeur!"

He threw back his head and laughed. "Is it a crime to have someone drive me around? I get a lot of work done while I'm traveling from one end of town to another."

"But can't you see I don't fit in? I'll never be the wife you need."

He moved quickly from his side of the booth to hers. She slid into the corner. His tall frame hovered over her. His eyes glinted.

"And what type of wife do I need?"

"A sophisticated woman. One that likes parties and socializing. That's not me. I'd make you miserable," Samantha said. Her breath caught in her throat. He surrounded her with his strong, masculine aura and the spicy male scent he wore. She both wanted to push him away and pull him forward. Her contrary thoughts had her confused.

He lifted her hand and turned it palm up. His lips brushed across her skin, shooting a needy hunger straight to her core.

"I want only you."

"Why?"

His lip curved into that sexy smile that made her heart trip. "I'll explain, later." His husky voice made her toes curl.

When his food arrived, he moved to the other side and ate quickly. Neither one said anything else. After paying the bill, he took her arm and led her to the car. "We'll be just in time.

They stopped in front of a nondescript building. A sign, Matthews and Company, hung on the wooden front door. Jackson rang the bell. Shortly, the door was opened by a burly man in a dark suit.

"Mr. Matthews is expecting you. Follow me." He led them down a well-lit, wide corridor and then into a bright room with cases of shiny jewelry. Paintings of nature, wild seas, a sunset over the desert, and other magnificent scenes were hung on the mahogany walls.

A tall, thin man with an equally thin mustache stepped forward to greet them. He reminded Samantha of an English butler. "It is good to see you, Mr. Stone. This must be your lovely fiancée."

"Yes, Mr. Matthews. This is Samantha Riley, soon to be Mrs. Stone."

"Welcome," Mr. Matthews greeted her and led them to a corner where two chairs sat on either side of a small Chippendale table.

Samantha glanced around. All the furniture appeared to be antiques. Soft music played in the background, and a teapot and two cups sat on the table beside a plate of brownies.

"Please help yourself. I will bring the choices I've picked out from your description of what you want. If none of them please Miss Riley, I'm sure we'll have others that will tempt her." Smiling, he bowed and walked briskly across the room and behind a long curtain.

"This is not like any jewelry store I've ever been in," Samantha said.

"Mr. Matthews has a select clientele," Jackson said. He was watching her closely.

"See what I mean. It's all this." She swung out her hands.

"Relax. Believe me, it will work out fine."

Samantha started to speak, but Mr. Matthews was back. He laid out a black velvet tray with at least ten rings sparkling against their background. She gasped at their beauty.

"Is there one specific ring you'd like to try?" Mr. Matthews asked.

She raised her eyes to Jackson. He studied her expression for a minute and then looked at the rings. "This one with the champagne diamonds and this more traditional one are my favorites. Which do you favor, Samantha?"

One ring had an oval champagne diamond in the center surrounded by two rows of regular diamonds. The other had a large round diamond surrounded by smaller round diamonds and baguettes on the side.

"They're both beautiful. You decide, Jackson."

"We'll take this one." He slid the champagne diamond ring onto her finger. "A perfect fit." Looking at her, he held her hand clasped tightly in his. "The color reminds me of your hair."

"Thank you, Mr. Matthews. Please have your assistant show Miss Riley to my car, and we'll take care of business."

"Certainly, this way Miss Riley."

"Don't forget to shop on the way home," Jackson said softly as she started to walk away. He pulled her to him and stooped to kiss her. "I'll expect more of a thank-you when I get home."

Shaken by his words, she hurried out of the room with the assistant, walking quickly to catch up with her.

Chapter Four

Samantha hung the dress she'd found, in a small shop near Jackson's townhouse, in the closet. She hoped she hadn't made a mistake. The dress caught her eye in the window and had fit perfectly. Still, she knew she was playing with fire. It wasn't a dress to go unnoticed. Shrugging, she gathered her underclothes and towel and headed to Jackson's shower. She thought she'd have plenty of time to have a quick wash in that gorgeous bathroom before he arrived.

She lathered her hair then stood, letting the warm water rinse over her head and flow along her body. A movement caught her eye. She stared as a naked Jackson opened the shower door to join her.

"I couldn't resist. You looked so delectable standing here like a water nymph with your back arched and water cascading over those curves."

Stunned, Samantha couldn't say a word. She hadn't seen him in a bathing suit in years, just jeans and cowboy shirts which hinted at but didn't show the six-pack, wide shoulders, and lean hips leading to a large cock pointed in her direction.

"Get out. We're not married yet." The low tone of her wavering voice didn't sound like she really wanted him to get out. In fact, a part of her wanted him to stay very much. Although she'd never given much thought to the idea of being naked with Jackson, suddenly she found herself unable to look away or move back from his enticing body.

His hands slid through her wet hair and pulled her face closer. "We will be, soon." His lips descended and ravished her mouth. This was the first intimate kiss they'd ever shared. Pressed wet and naked against Jackson as he kissed her senseless, her body melted against his rock-hard muscles. His tongue tangled with hers, while his arms held her snug. His cock caught between them. There was no doubt to what he had in mind. It was sex. To her surprise, she realized she craved him as much as he appeared to desire her. Perhaps sex with Jackson would be different. He slid one of his hands across her side to her breast, and his thumb rubbed her nipple, while his other hand rubbed across her buttocks. The sheer delight of Jackson's hands caressing her body made all of Samantha's thoughts fly straight out of her head.

All her awareness was centered on the man holding her, his heated body, and the needy feeling growing inside her. His lips left her mouth and trailed across one cheek. He soon nibbled on her earlobe, and then kissed the skin between her neck and shoulder. His cock throbbed against her hip each time his lips pressed to her skin. Her pussy gushed with the need he aroused with only several well-placed kisses. She wanted him more and more. His fingers moved down to her lower lips and caressed her clit. She threw her head back and moaned. Hunger flashed through her.

He reached to the side of the shower and opened a condom package. In her surprise, she'd never noticed him put it there. She watched while he quickly put it on, silently urging him to hurry.

"Open your legs and put your arms around my neck," he said. Then he picked her up and wrapped her legs around his waist. Holding her with one arm, he moved his cock to the very wet slit of her pussy and started to enter.

Samantha's inner walls throbbed with desire. She moved to accommodate his large cock, and he pushed all the way inside her body. She tightened around him, enticing him to sink even deeper. Her mouth clamped on his. She sucked on his tongue while he pushed her to the tile wall and took her slow and easy, almost drawing all the way out before sinking his wide cock in deeper. Sensitive nerves she'd never known she had pulsed for more. His hand slipped between them as he found her clit, again. Each stroke across the sensitive nub, as he pushed his cock to the end of her pussy, was gloriously driving her pleasure higher and higher. His breath came in gasps against her throat, and each penetration of his cock sent tingles like lightning bolts through her body. She met his every thrust even as he moved faster and faster. Finally the ache exploded into unbelievable euphoria. Almost immediately, he pushed his cock hard and deep one last time. She heard him yell her name right before he stiffened and fell against her.

Gasping for breath, she glanced around and saw their intertwined bodies reflected back to her from several directions. Jackson's tan skin next to her slightly paler complexion, his golden-brown hair shining in the glow from the overhead light. Gradually, he let her legs slide to the shower floor. He bent his head.

"Are you all right?"

She laid her head against his chest where his heart still pounded. After taking several more deep breaths, she looked at him. "I think so."

He smiled. "Now you look much more like a happily engaged woman."

"Is that what this was about? Getting me ready to impress your friends with how crazy I am about you?" She glared at him.

"What do you think?" He picked up the soap from the floor and began to wash his body. "I'll finish quickly and let you have the room to yourself." He turned to rinse and soon stepped out, drying and wrapping a towel around his middle. He walked to the door. "I'll shave after you've gone to your room. By the way, there is a private bath connected to your bedroom, in case you didn't notice. Don't use mine again unless you want a repeat performance."

Samantha shivered even with the warm water flowing over her heated body. She wanted to cry but blinked the tears back. Totally confused by her body's response and not wanting to admit she wanted more of him, she blanked the thoughts out of her mind and hurried to finish.

* * * *

Jackson pulled on his jeans and went into his study. He needed a good stiff drink. After pouring bourbon into his glass, he prowled around the room. He hadn't meant to move so quickly. He'd been planning on giving her more time. Still, when he saw her in the shower, her body reflected on the various mirrors, his brains cells burned up and all attention went to his pulsing, hungry cock.

He'd have stopped if she'd said no. She didn't. Her soft curves molded to his body. Her mouth, sweet as candy kisses, increased his hunger tenfold. And when he slid into her hot, wet pussy and she clamped tighter around him, he thought he'd died or was going to the way his heart pounded.

She wanted him. She just wasn't ready to admit her feelings. She was his. He'd never let her out of her bargain. She might as well get used to it. He heard his bedroom door open and her door shut.

His cock had hardened at the mere thought of her. He'd been waiting for her to leave his room. If he'd seen her naked again, even partially, he didn't trust himself not to take her to bed and ravish that delectable body one more time. He'd better go dress for the dinner.

Thirty minutes later, he knocked on her door.

"I'll be right out."

Samantha opened the door, and his breath caught somewhere between his chest and throat. She wore a bronze-colored cocktail dress that clung to every sweet curve and came close to matching her sherry-colored eyes. High-necked and long-sleeved, it hinted at what seductive pleasures lay underneath. The skirt flared just above her knees. Gold sandal heels completed the outfit. He raised his head to look at her shiny fall of golden hair that curled around her face and down over her shoulders.

"I'm afraid all the wonderful makeup that the lady applied to make me look good came off in the shower." She blushed and looked down.

His finger tipped her face up. "You look beautiful with makeup or without." His fingers ran through the silk strands of hair. "Let's go over to your mirror. I have something to add to your outfit." She hesitated before turning and walking briskly across the room to the dresser. He held in his gasp. Her dress was backless all the way to the slight curve above her sexy derriere. Hot desire kicked him in the stomach. He was almost afraid to touch her for fear he'd go right up in smoke.

She glanced at him. "Do you like my dress?"

"Too much. I'm afraid I'll have to beat off the men when you walk into the private dining room downstairs." He stepped behind her and brushed her hair aside to place a chain around her neck. He handed her a box with matching earrings.

Her hand brushed across the cool, oval diamond where it lay just between her breasts. "I can't accept such an expensive gift."

He kissed the side of her forehead. "Of course you can. People will expect to see such gifts to my fiancée from me. You do want this to appear to be a regular engagement, don't you?"

"Of course, but..."

Placing his hands on her shoulders, he moved his body closer. "We will be married. *You* proposed, and I accepted. Your grandfather expects it. Will you disappoint him? Or me?"

* * * *

Samantha stood in the doorway of the large dining room. "Why did you say you're giving this dinner?" she asked Jackson.

"With all the excitement during my trip home, I'd forgotten about it. This is a thank you to business partners and an enticement to prospective clients. My staff will be working the room. Here comes another of my senior associates." Jackson nodded his head toward a tall, statuesque redheaded woman, who made a beeline toward them.

"Jackson, I'm glad to see you back from the wilds of the country." She purred the words from between ruby red lips. Her skintight, sparkling blue gown showed every curve, clearly.

"Lunette, I'd like you to meet my fiancée, Samantha Riley."

If Samantha hadn't been watching closely, she'd have missed the blink and shocked look quickly covered with a smile. Lunette put out her hand to Samantha.

"How nice to meet you, and aren't you the lucky lady. I didn't believe he'd"—she moved her head toward Jackson—"ever marry. How did you get the words *marry me* out of his mouth?"

"I proposed to him."

This time the woman couldn't hide her surprise. Jackson laughed. "She's telling the truth. Of course since I've known her for years, and wanted all along to marry her, I accepted."

Samantha turned to him in shock. He bent his head to her and gave her a quick kiss.

"I hate to break up this cozy moment, but the representative from Singapore needs to speak with you." She took Jackson's arm. "If you'll excuse us," she said as she pulled on Jackson's arm.

"Do you want to come with us?" Jackson asked.

"No. I'll wander around the room. Go, do your business." In truth, she was relieved to have some distance from him. Ever since the shower encounter and then the gift—her hand touched the necklace—she'd been feeling off kilter. Her body reacted to his slightest brush against her. Desire had shimmered through her when his fingers touched the nape of her neck when he fastened the chain.

She began to slowly skirt the outside of the room. Couples stood in small groups talking, while waiters circulated around them to offer drinks and appetizers. Samantha wished she could transport herself back to her bedroom at the ranch and be standing at her window looking out at the stars. Here she felt uncomfortable and out of place.

"What is the most beautiful woman in the room doing standing alone?" A tall man with blond hair and a dimpled smile greeted her carrying two wineglasses. He handed one to Samantha. "You look like you need a drink to get in the party mood."

"And you appointed yourself my rescuer?"

"I did. I'm Scott Perkins."

"Do you work for Jackson?" she asked. She took a sip of the white wine and studied Scott's face. He looked too soft, and his quick smile didn't fool her. He wasn't Jackson's friend.

"No. Jackson and I don't work together or play well with each other." Scott wrapped an arm around her shoulder and started to walk her toward the open sliding glass doors.

Samantha stiffened. "Take your arm off of me," she snapped.

"Honey, I'm just trying to be friendly."

"Be friendly somewhere else, Perkins." Jackson stepped between Scott and Samantha. "She's my future wife. Touch her again, and I'll flatten you."

Scott put up his hands in mock fear. "Whoa, a woman that has gotten under your skin." He laughed. "I'll wait. You get easily bored."

Jackson pulled back his arm, but Samantha grabbed it. "Don't, this is silly. I can take care of myself. I'd managed all right before you arrived." Jackson turned his head and frowned at her, but he stepped back.

"See you later, honey." Scott waved, a taunting grin on his face.

"He doesn't like you."

"No, he inherited his dad's companies and has been a thorn in my side ever since."

"Why invite him to your dinner party?"

"Because that saying about keeping your enemies close is true. It's always best to keep an eye on characters like Scott. Come on, I'll introduce you to some of the friendlier people in this gathering."

Samantha tried to remember names, but after the first few, they all ran together. She did notice all the younger women smiled and flirted with Jackson even after he told them about their engagement. Obviously, they didn't believe it would last either. Neither did

Samantha. This was so much Jackson's world and not hers at all.

She slipped away from Jackson's side while he and several men discussed business. After asking for directions, she headed to the ladies' room. As the rest of the building, it was large and ornate. She entered into a sitting room with chairs covered in flowered material and light blue walls. A tea and coffee pot sat on a round table to the right alongside a platter of chocolate chip cookies.

The room invited her to sit and relax. She poured a cup of tea and put two chocolate chip cookies on a small plate then sat in one of the large, soft chairs. She'd just bitten into her cookie when the door opened.

"I thought I might find you here." Lunette sauntered into the room and clicked the lock behind her. She poured a cup of coffee and sat across from Samantha. "This gives us an opportunity to talk privately."

"Do we have something to discuss?"

"Don't act the innocent with me." She ran her eyes over Samantha. "You may think he'll marry you. He won't. He doesn't know it, but he's mine. I haven't worked the past three years to become invaluable to him to lose him to some baby doll blonde. You're a dime a dozen, as the old saying goes."

"But I wear his ring." Samantha flashed the stones under the bright lights. Anger and jealousy shone on Lunette's face.

"You'll see. I travel with him. I've been waiting for the right time to seduce him. Seems I almost waited too long." She stood and went to the door. "And I don't plan to be fair about this, so don't get too used to that ring."

Samantha listened to her high heels as they clicked across the floor when Lunette stalked away. The door shut with a quiet swish, shutting out the sound. Samantha shuddered. Lunette intended to make this a battle between them. She should be glad. If she and Jackson broke up because of another woman, Gramps would comfort her and surely take away his demands. Lunette might be the answer to her problem.

She took a sip of her cold tea and put it down. The thought of Lunette with Jackson made her heart shudder just a bit. She needed to go home to regain her balance and think more clearly. Tomorrow she'd demand Jackson return her to the ranch, no excuses or other ideas for outings.

After setting her cup aside and throwing away the remaining cookie, she stopped at the full-length mirror by the door and noticed her pale cheeks and troubled expression. She had only one more worry—she still had to get through tonight alone in the apartment with Jackson. She'd never had difficulty resisting a man's advances. Not until now. She didn't want to care about him. After her parents' deaths, she'd never allowed anyone to become too close, except for her grandparents. And something told her letting Jackson get close was the most dangerous of all. She'd better rejoin the group. Somehow she'd manage to get through the night, and then demand to go home bright and early tomorrow.

Chapter Five

"I'm not sending you home alone. I'd planned on going with you and staying for several days. On Thursday I have to travel to Singapore and won't be back for a week. The next few days will give us time to enjoy the outdoors and each other."

"Jackson, we need some time apart. This has all happened too fast. You saw what a failure I was at the dinner. I hate socializing, and I do it poorly," Samantha said.

"Nonsense. Everyone was charmed by you. Anyway, you aren't going to change my mind. I've arranged for the helicopter to pick us up."

"I suppose you have a rooftop landing area here, too."

He cupped his hands around her face. "Yes, I do. Quit finding fault with my conveniences and enjoy them. Now, go get your bag and we'll head to the roof."

Samantha did as he said and followed him up the steps to the rooftop. The flight home went smooth and seemed quicker than the ride to town. Jackson had brought along some paperwork, so there was little conversation. He glanced up once to check on her. Although butterflies bounced in her stomach, Samantha had refused to let her fear show.

Just sitting close to him sent desire coursing along her veins. She had no intention of touching him. Thank goodness last night he'd excused himself shortly after they returned to his townhouse. He'd disappeared into his study.

She'd lain awake for what seemed hours, listening for any sounds from across the hall. Finally, she heard him come out the door and close it. Her body tensed, wondering if he'd look in on her. She'd let her breath out in relief when nothing happened. She was ready to be at home where she'd be able to sort out all these new sensations happening in her body.

"Are you going to get out?" Jackson stood outside the helicopter door with his hand out.

"Oh, yes. Thank you." She took his hand and sighed in relief when her feet touched the ground.

"I'll drive you to your grandfather's," Jackson said. "We'll get together tonight at my place for dinner."

"I don't know if Gramps will want to go out to dinner."

"I don't want him to. This is you and me, no one else."

His deep tone brought her gaze to his. His hungry look shook her. She found herself staring at his mouth, wanting to lean against him and raise her lips to his.

"Keep looking at me like that and I'll take you home with me right now." His husky voice poured over her like smooth silk. Every nerve in her yelled *yes!*

Samantha took two steps back. "Tonight's not good. We need some alone time."

"That's exactly what I'm suggesting."

"You know what I mean. We need time away from each other."

"I don't agree, and your grandfather will be suspicious if we aren't anxious to be together."

"So this is just to convince Gramps we're serious?"

"You wouldn't want him to think you'd made all this up to trick him?"

Samantha took a deep breath. "All right."

"I'll pick you up at seven, and do try to look a little more pleased."

He helped her into his truck and drove straight to her ranch. "I won't come in." He opened the door for her. "See you at seven." She picked up her bag, waved, and hurried inside.

Shadows and cool air greeted her. The house was unusually quiet. "Maria," Samantha called out. When she didn't answer, Samantha wandered through the kitchen to the back screen door and spotted Maria gathering beans in a large bowl. She raised her head when Samantha came out the door.

"You're back." A large smile covered her face. "Let me see that engagement ring. I can see the sparkles from here." Maria headed toward her, and Samantha held out her hand.

"My, my. It's beautiful and impressive." She looked at Samantha. "Do you like it?"

Did she? Samantha studied her ring. Sunlight sent flashes of light glancing off the stones. "It is lovely," she said in a low tone. "But, I'm glad to be back. The big city is not for me."

Maria opened the door and went into the kitchen. She took the bowl to the sink and started running water over the vegetables.

"Guess you'll have to get used to spending time there. Don't expect Jackson will want his wife in one place and him in another."

"How do you know what Jackson might or might not want?" Samantha asked as she took out a pitcher of tea and poured herself a glass. "Want some tea?"

Maria shook her head no and continued to work on the beans. After a moment, she said, "He's a man. No man wants to have his woman miles away from where he's living. Not natural."

His woman, the image of those words brought an instant recall of the hungry look she'd seen on Jackson's face earlier. A part of her was trying very hard to keep control of the situation, but she found it harder and harder to deny the urges of her body, the desire to have Jackson make love to her again. And yet, she feared if she gave in to him, she'd soon become more Mrs. Stone and less the woman she had envisioned for herself.

"What do you want for dinner?" Maria asked. "I thought I might cook a couple of steaks?"

"I'm going to Jackson's for dinner."

Maria chuckled. "See, he's a typical man."

Samantha felt her blush. "It's only dinner, Maria."

"Whatever you say, dear. I'll ask Mr. Riley what he'd like."

"Where is Gramps?"

A brief frown crossed Maria's face. "He said he had an important appointment in Saddle Creek. He didn't say with whom or how soon he'd return."

"You're worried."

"No. I'm sure it's nothing. Now you go unpack and decide on what you'll wear for your big date tonight."

"Really, Maria, you and Gramps are too much." She heard Maria laugh as she headed upstairs. Gramps rarely went to town. Folks mostly came to him. Maria was worried, although she denied it. Something felt wrong. Still, whatever the problem, if there was one, Maria would never tell her if Gramps said not to.

She quickly unpacked and changed into her jeans and a blue shirt. Just the outfit alone made her feel more like her old self. She'd saddle Princess and ride around the ranch. She opened her window and took a deep breath. Home. This was where she belonged, where she intended to stay. She just hadn't figured out how to make it all happen her way.

* * * *

Samantha took a last glance in the mirror at her jeans and black shirt. She'd pulled her hair back into a pony tail. Casual and comfortable, nothing special to give Jackson any ideas. *And how about your own?* She shook her head at her reflection. She had herself under control. What happened in Houston was just an aberration.

She walked briskly downstairs and heard voices from the kitchen. Gramps, Jackson, and Maria sat around the table drinking coffee and talking. Jackson spotted her first. He glanced at his watch.

"A woman that's ready on time, a miracle." He gave her that

thousand-watt smile, and her knees went weak.

Ignoring him, she went to Gramps and kissed his cheek. "I missed you today."

"I had lunch with some friends and went out to see old Mrs. Daley. Her arthritis keeps her close to home." He nodded at Jackson. "He tells me he's having you over for dinner."

"We discussed it, but we can eat here just as well and keep you company."

"Definitely not. Maria is going to join me. I'll be fine. You two have a lot of talking to do. Jackson said he'd like to decide on a wedding date, and I'm all for that. Don't keep this old man waiting too long. I still want to walk you down the aisle."

Samantha saw the warmth in Gramps eyes, so she bit her tongue. She'd been planning on a long engagement, but looking at Jackson and Gramps, she didn't think she'd get away with prolonging the inevitable.

Jackson rose, kissed Maria on the cheek, and shook Gramps' hand. He put his arm around Samantha. "Don't wait up for her. It might take hours to convince her to plan our marriage for later this month."

"This month!"

"We'll talk later." Jackson shuffled her quickly out the back door and to his truck. Before she said another word, he helped her into the seat and went around the front to get into the driver's side.

"I'm not marrying you this month. There are plans to be made, invitations to send out. Why, you probably have hundreds that will expect an invite."

He reached out with his right hand and squeezed her leg. "Relax. We'll discuss the wedding while I barbecue our steaks."

"Right. You don't discuss. You order. I will not be told what to do."

His deep chuckle and the warmth of his hand on her thigh sent a zing of desire straight to her core. She would not let him distract her with sex. She straightened in her seat and brushed his hand aside. "Behave. I'm coming for dinner, not to be dinner."

Jackson laughed out loud. "That does sound much more enticing than mere barbecue."

"Whatever has come over you, Jackson?"

"You, and the thought of having you all to myself, especially on our honeymoon."

Heat rushed to Samantha's face. "We do not need a honeymoon." She heard the tremble in her voice. Jackson's words had conjured all kinds of erotic pictures. Maybe she was losing her mind from all this stress. Determined to ignore him for the rest of the short ride, she turned her head and studied the passing scenery. Jackson hummed as he drove. She found she couldn't ignore him or put him out of her thoughts. His scent, particular to him—part outdoorsy and part just his sheer masculinity—surrounded her, his humming set her nerves on edge, and his body seemed to fill up the truck cabin. Damn him. Where had all her newfound determination gone?

"Make yourself comfortable," Jackson said as he led her into the large family room with the kitchen on one side. "I'll start the fire. The steaks are marinating in the refrigerator."

"Can I help?"

"Sure, toss a salad together and turn on the oven." He pointed to the island in the center of the kitchen. "The potatoes are ready to go in."

Samantha saw the aluminum foil-wrapped spuds. In the fridge she found romaine lettuce, radishes, tomatoes, shredded carrots, and mushrooms to dice and slice for the salad bowl. Jackson had gone out the glass doors to the patio and was bent over checking the propane tank.

He really did have a fine ass. His tight jeans did nothing to hide his physique. He'd left his white shirt unbuttoned to the third hole, and brown hair shown between the edges. A familiar gold chain hung around his neck. She had glanced closer, when she first noticed it, and it was the one she'd given him at his high school graduation. A St. Christopher's medal to protect him in his travels. On the back she'd had inscribed, *To My Best Friend ever, Samantha.*

Thinking back to their interlude in the shower, she realized he'd worn it then, too. Had he always kept it on or just recently since their situation changed? She could ask him, but something stopped her. She didn't want to know.

"You're staring," Jackson said in a teasing tone.

"Not at you," she denied. "My thoughts were miles away."

"Your nose is going to start growing if you keep telling fibs."

"I don't fib." Samantha turned her back to him and put the potatoes in the oven then grabbed the vegetables and began to rinse and cut them up. *Concentrate, be strong, or you'll find yourself at the justice of the peace tomorrow.*

Surprisingly, Jackson didn't tease her anymore, and he kept the conversation casual.

"The food is delicious," Samantha said. "I've noticed you've made some changes since you bought the ranch from your folks. I like the new colors in here." She glanced around the family room. "And that's a gorgeous pool and patio area, very private, too, with the high concrete walls you had built around it."

Jackson grinned. "That's so I can skinny-dip whenever I want. Have you ever gone skinny-dipping, Samantha?"

There went her face blushing again. "No, I haven't."

"What a shame. Maybe we can take care of that tonight. Your first adult adventure with me."

Samantha jumped up and began to clear the table. "I don't think so, Jackson."

He stopped her, took the dishes, and set them in the sink. "The maid comes tomorrow. She'll clean this up." He pulled her close to him. "I dare you."

"No."

"Scared?"

"Of course not."

"How about if I promise not to do anything you don't want." His husky tone flowed like a caress over her body. "If it makes you feel better, then leave on your bra and panties."

"But you'll be naked."

"Of course." Slowly, he lowered his head and captured her lips. His tongue slid into the warm recesses of her mouth, moving in a light, soothing motion. He continued to kiss her while he picked her up and carried her outside to the pool. After putting her down, he strode to the side of the patio, reached in the family room door, and flipped the switch, leaving the house in darkness. Next he put out the lights on the patio and around the pool, except for a few colored ones under the water.

"Just in case you decide to join me. You can be assured no one will see you but me." His hand went to his shirt. He quickly took it off, and then sat and removed his shoes.

Samantha watched, mesmerized, as he undid the button on his jeans and slid the zipper down. Her heart pounded. She ought to turn away, but her fascination held her in place. Jackson stepped out of his jeans and shorts. Moonlight glistened across the planes of his chest and abdomen. His face was in the shadows, so all she saw was the taunting curve of his mouth. Walking casually to the deep end, he dove into the water and came up shaking sparkling drops of water from his hair that appeared black in the dim light.

"Are you going to stand there all night or join me?"

"Turn around."

"Not fair, you watched me."

"Please, Jackson."

He moved away from the edge and began to swim along the length of the pool. Samantha undressed quickly, leaving her bra and panties on, then she slipped into the pool from the nearest side. Jackson popped up right in front of her.

"Now that wasn't so hard, was it?"

"I don't guess so." She plunged to his left and swam away. They raced each other from one end of the pool to the other. Samantha swam well, but the only time she beat Jackson, she knew he'd held up just a bit. Breathless, she stopped at the end and paddled with her feet. Jackson moved to her side.

"Ready to get out? If so, I have a suggestion."

Samantha raised her eyebrow. "I'm afraid to ask what it is."

"Nothing terrible. I'll give you a towel, and while you remove your wet underclothes, I'll get some lotion and give you a massage."

"That sounds dangerous. I'll be nude."

"Darling, I've seen you nude before, and I said I won't do anything you don't want me to."

Her heart tripped faster. She started to say no, to take her home, but found the words spilling out of her mouth were just the opposite. "All right. Still, you will stop if I say so."

He didn't wait for her to change her mind. He handed her a towel from the cabana, situated at the darkest end of the patio, then went inside. She barely had time to wrap the towel around her before he returned with a large bottle of lotion. He took her arm and directed her to a double-sized lounge chair. It was wide and long.

"Lie down on your stomach."

Samantha managed to lie down without dropping her towel. Jackson straddled her and pulled her wet hair to the side. Soon, she felt his hands filled with lotion begin to massage her neck and shoulders.

"Relax. You're full of tense knots."

How did any woman relax with a nude man straddling them and his warm hands doing wonderful things to her muscles and skin? He kneaded away all the aches and tension as he moved along each arm and then took long strokes over her back. When he got to the towel, he lifted her enough to pull it off her backside.

She had a fleeting thought to protest, but he hadn't left her the energy to move, much less say anything but moan in pleasure. When his strong hands caressed her buttocks, fluid seeped out of her pussy and fire licked along every nerve in her body. She started to move around.

"Stay still. I'm not through yet, my love. I'm just getting started."

Jackson slid further down and massaged each thigh and leg before continuing to her feet. His fingers slid lotion over her toes and instep. When he rubbed her feet, any lingering tension flowed away. He left her feet and did a quick rub up her body until he wrapped his body around her.

"I'm going to turn you and continue on your front," he whispered in her ear then nibbled on her earlobe.

Low inside, an ache began to build. She gave no resistance as he moved off of her and rolled her to face him. His hunger made his face look drawn. His lowered eyelids hid their expression. A cool breeze rippled across her skin, causing her to shiver.

He straddled her again, wiped the lotion from his hands, and began to massage her scalp. "I love your hair. When it's dry, the strands flow through my fingers like silk."

Lowering his head, he kissed her cheeks, the corners of her mouth, and sucked on her lower lip. His hands moved to her neck and shoulders, caressing her while his tongue tasted and teased her mouth.

Continuing his exploration, he nuzzled her neck. "I can feel your pulse beating against my lips. You smell like flowers and taste like the sweetest nectar." His husky voice made her ache.

He had her almost breathless as his body and hands circled her, becoming an extension of herself. His teasing tongue tasted her belly button and licked her skin to her pussy lips. She raised her hips to meet him, but he surprised her by changing positions and pouring cool lotion on her feet to restart his massage.

Her whole body throbbed and hungered for him. She wanted him inside her. She moaned, twisting around.

His deep chuckle only aroused her more. "Be still. I'm not done."

Heat flowed upwards from her feet to touch every overly

sensitized inch of her body. He kissed each toe and her instep, taking what seemed like forever. It was heavenly, and yet she wanted, needed more.

Finally, he began to kiss her ankle, lower leg, and then he rubbed more lotion on her thighs and began to massage her, especially along the inner thigh.

She stared up at the sprinkling of stars above and the slender curve of the moon. Vaguely, she heard a rip as he opened the condom package. Quickly, he moved back to her, and his lips ran across her clit, arousing her to a fever pitch. He separated her pussy lips and tasted and touched all her most intimate places. Her insides clenched and unclenched, starving for his attention. She raised herself and opened her legs further, moaning the words, "fill me, please fill me."

He moved up the length of her, where he could lick her peaked nipple. His fingers reached down and stroked just inside the opening to her wet, tight pussy. In her impatience, she took hold of his warm, stiff cock, and moving his hand away, she positioned him right at her opening.

"Do you want me to make love to you?"

"Yes, yes, push inside of me. I can't wait another second."

His cock slipped, just barely, into her gushing, wet pussy, and then he rubbed his thumb over her clit. Samantha raised her hips and pulled his buttocks toward her, but he controlled their progress, holding back and entering inch by inch until her head thrashed from side to side.

"Say you want me again. I want to hear the words."

"I want you, damn it."

He plunged his wide cock in all the way and ravaged her mouth while his body thrust in and out, taking her to a level of pleasure she'd never known. His kiss muffled her scream as she exploded with tremors rocketing through her limbs. A few more strokes and he pushed in hard one last time. His body stiffened as he crushed her to him.

Gradually, the shaky world settled. Jackson lay on her, breathing heavily. He pushed himself up with his arms and stared down at her. "You're all right?"

Samantha's heart still pounded in her chest, but she nodded her head yes. Another second and Jackson rolled off of her.

"You will marry me on Saturday, two weeks from now. Invite whoever you want, big wedding or a justice of the peace, I don't care."

She wanted to remind him she wasn't always going to take orders, but at this point she had no energy or desire to say anything. When reality returned, she blushed at the thought that she'd forgotten they were outside, even if behind high walls. Also, all her plans to resist him had melted away at his touch.

He rose and pulled on his jeans. "I'd better drive you home. Otherwise I'll end up keeping you here all night." She put out her hand, and he pulled her to him, gave her a quick hug, and kissed the top of her head. He reached for her clothes. "I'll help you dress."

"Oh no. I'm quite capable of dressing myself. Go inside and give me some privacy. I'll join you in a moment."

Jackson started to say something, but instead, he strode across the patio to the door. "Don't take too long."

Samantha took a deep breath and dove into the pool. The cool water dissipated the heat from her body. She swam two laps before getting out, drying off, and dressing. Jackson had come to the door.

"Ready?"

"Yes." But she doubted it. Would she ever be ready for all the changes swamping her every day since she'd asked Jackson to marry her? Jackson had been her best friend for years. She'd known him better than any other man. *She thought.*

Yet, the man who accepted her proposal seemed a different entity. *I don't know him at all.*

Chapter Six

Jackson glanced at Samantha several times as he drove her back to her ranch. Inside the truck, the silence was thick with unsaid words. He pulled close to the porch and turned off the engine. Outside, an owl hooted in the distance and several dogs barked.

"Are you angry about what happened tonight?" The words came out before he thought about them. Had he pushed too fast? His own strong desire had no patience. He'd not even tried to pull back.

Samantha glanced at him. "Not angry, confused, tired." A brief smile crossed her face. "I'm totally relaxed in a different way."

His lips curling into a satisfied smile went unnoticed. "Let's go riding tomorrow or, I should say, today. We'll talk."

"I'll think about it. Call me later." Samantha opened her door. "Don't get out. I know my way in."

He waited until she disappeared inside before starting his truck and heading home. Her scent clung to him and was in the air around him. She excited him in a way no other woman had. He'd known for a long time he wanted to marry her. He'd never dreamed of the intense desire she'd release in him.

Tonight, he'd taken her slowly at first and then fast and hard, a raging fever of need and want taking control. Jackson raked his fingers through his hair. He'd always been a controlled man in his business and personal life. She'd brought out a side of him he'd never experienced before.

He wanted Samantha more than anything or anyone he'd ever desired. She'd marry him. She cared for him, and hopefully she loved him, but loving meant letting go of control, and for Samantha that was difficult. Still, whatever means he had to use, he was not going to lose her.

* * * *

Her ringing phone woke her. "Hello."

"It's time to wake up, sleepyhead," Jackson said.

Samantha looked at her clock. "Ten. I've got to get dressed. I never sleep this late."

"Get ready. We'll go riding."

"I'm not even awake yet, and I have to check with Gramps to see which part of the ranch he's working today."

"Your grandfather stopped by early. He's headed out to his south field. I sent one of my men with him so you wouldn't feel you had to help."

"Jackson, I really don't like this attitude you have that you can control my life."

"We need to plan our wedding. I'm going to call my folks after we talk and make some decisions. I thought you'd like to speak with them. It's your choice. I have plenty of work around here I can do. In fact, that might be the best idea. You can think about what kind of wedding you want to have, and what we need to do to get ready in two weeks. We'll go riding tomorrow."

She hadn't really wanted him to change their plans. Her annoyance at him arrogantly taking control had backfired on her. But this would give her time alone to build up her defenses. Really, she had to stop melting into a puddle at his feet.

"All right, tomorrow is better."

"Good. I'll ride over around seven in the morning in time to have breakfast with your grandfather." He hung up.

Samantha stared at the phone and shook her head to wake up better. She'd gotten her way, but it didn't feel good. Not at all.

She dressed in her old jeans and a comfortable shirt, pulled on her cowboy boots, and grabbed her hat then headed downstairs.

"Good morning, Maria. When will Gramps return?"

"Not sure. He didn't say."

Samantha took a biscuit off a platter by the stove. "I'll eat this on the way. I'm going to join him."

"He thought you and Jackson were riding out together."

"Nope. We both have our own things to do. See you later."

Her mare, Princess, let Samantha know she wanted to run. Samantha enjoyed flying across the meadow with the breeze in her face and sunshine beaming down on her. She'd returned to her element, nothing but trees, cattle, and open land stretching as far as she could see. The fragrance of wildflowers tickled her nose. In the distance, she saw several of the ranch hands working on a fence. Gramps sat on his horse observing them. She pulled Princess up and headed in their direction.

Seeing her, Gramps rode toward her. "Thought Jackson and you had plans for the day."

"Nope. We both had things we wanted to do separately." Samantha took a deep breath. "I've missed being out on the ranch. Even a few days in the big city is too much for me."

Gramps frowned. "You know your life will change when you get married."

"Not really. Jackson's agreed I can take care of the two ranches while he does what he needs to around the world." She shrugged. "He's headed to Singapore on Thursday."

"I don't think so. He said he'd made plans for someone else to cover for him."

"Whatever. Today is mine to enjoy what I love doing. Are you staying out here all day?" she asked Gramps.

"No. I'm heading back."

"Don't worry. I'll be here to help. See you at dinner, Gramps." She pretended not to notice the scowl on his face as he rode off.

In the late afternoon, a cooler breeze blowing over Samantha's face had her looking up. Dark, cumulous clouds were building in the east. She and the others decided to head for home. The breeze soon turned into a strong wind, and large raindrops began to fall just as they reached the barn. Samantha led Princess inside and removed her saddle and rubbed her down.

She was tired, a good tired, and she hadn't thought of Jackson at all—well, almost not at all. Having a day by herself had given her back her equilibrium. She'd not be a pushover for him tomorrow. Feeling very satisfied, Samantha walked briskly through the rain toward the back screen door.

"Sam." Maria opened the door calling her name. Samantha ran to her and took the towel she offered. "Jackson wants to speak with you." Maria pointed to the receiver hanging from the wall phone. Samantha wrapped the towel around her wet hair and picked up the receiver. "Jackson?"

"Did you have a busy day?"

"Busy, but good."

"Look, something has come up. I'm flying out early tomorrow morning, but I plan to be back by late tomorrow evening. I'm going to have several of my associates and their families join me here for the weekend. I thought you might think about how we could entertain them and their children. My PR person is working on some ideas, but if you have any suggestions I'll see they get added."

"Have any of them been to a ranch before?" Samantha asked.

"Not the families. Most of my senior associates have been here for a working retreat."

"If I think of anything, I'll give you a call."

"Good. I've got to go. Oh, by the way, have you given our wedding any thought?"

"Not really, and with the rest of this week being so busy, we'll need to put it off for at least another week or two."

He laughed. "Not at all. I'll ask Mrs. Haverty to come here with the rest of the staff. She can help you plan."

"That won't be necessary. I'll invite Janice. She's very organized."

"All right. Talk with you tomorrow night." The phone clicked off. Samantha glanced around. Maria had left the kitchen to give her privacy. For some reason, her good mood had evaporated. Surely, she hadn't been looking forward to their ride tomorrow that much. She was tired. A hot shower and meal and she'd be fine. Afterwards she'd call Janice, and tomorrow she'd work with the ranch hands again. Somehow that didn't excite her as much as it had this morning.

* * * *

Jackson strode into his office early the next morning. He'd missed seeing Samantha yesterday but hoped a few days apart might help her realize she did want to marry him, and not just because of her grandfather's demands.

He really did need to be here in the city today. He had papers to sign, and soon he'd have to make a final decision on his replacement. He planned to retire the day before his wedding. He'd still be the major stockholder and president of the board.

All the necessary decisions and plans were coming together. He'd decided on this move six months ago, when he realized he wanted to be more actively involved with all aspects of ranching and the community. He'd tired of the cutthroat rat race.

One of the reasons he'd never seriously considered marriage until now was because he didn't want to raise a family in that environment. He wanted his full-time home and job to be at the ranch. He'd get to see his children grow, to teach them to ride a horse and to work the farm.

Only a very select few knew about the major changes coming. He'd decided even to wait to tell Samantha. It was vitally important that not even a hint get out until all papers had been signed. His enemies might like to create problems.

"Hello, Mrs. Haverty. How are you today?" Jackson smiled at his longtime secretary.

"I'm fine, Mr. Stone. Mr. Terrell is in your office enjoying a cup of coffee."

"He's always said you make the best," Jackson teased. He strode to his door and stopped. "Mrs. Haverty, I'd like you to come in after he leaves. I have something I want to ask you."

She looked puzzled. "Is anything wrong?"

"Not at all, just the opposite. We'll talk later." He waved and went in to join one of his best friends, who also happened to be his attorney.

Jackson hurried through the day. He'd decided to get back early enough to visit Samantha. His strong desire to see her and touch her continued to surprise him. The big question was, did she miss him as much?

By five, he was on his helicopter headed home. Mrs. Haverty had agreed to think about his offer to join him at the ranch as his all-around assistant with the business of running the ranch. She'd voiced her preference for the country several times in his presence, so he expected, if her husband agreed, that they'd move to the ranch shortly after him. She'd known all along of his plans to retire and leave most of the running of his company to one of his current associates.

He still hadn't quite decided which one he'd choose. For that reason, he had invited them and their families to visit this weekend. He hoped to convince Samantha to be his hostess.

"Let me off at the Rileys' landing strip," he said to his pilot.

"Yes, Sir." The pilot turned the bird due west as Jackson settled back in his seat. At his feet was his surprise for Samantha.

* * * *

Samantha heard the helicopter coming close. She leaned as far as she could out her window and saw the big bird landing. Her heartbeat quickened. Jackson must have left the city early. She'd just hung up from talking with Janice and arranging her arrival for Friday. Glancing down at her shorts and T-shirt, she started to the closet to change, but the noise outside had stopped, meaning Jackson was probably already coming to the house. She put on her tan sandals and hurried downstairs.

His large frame shadowed the doorway as she reached the last step. "Samantha," he called out.

"I'm here. Just a minute." She took a deep breath to steady her nerves before forcing herself to walk slowly to the screen door. "Jackson, I thought you weren't returning until late tonight." She opened the door and stood back as he came in, carrying a carton.

"My work took less time than I expected." He dipped his head and kissed her mouth. "Miss me?" His eyes held a teasing expression.

"Not at all," she said. "The time went by very fast."

"Liar," he whispered in her ear.

The brown box he held in his hands moved. She heard a noise. "What is that?"

He held it out to her. "My surprise."

"For me?" Her face flushed with pleasure.

He nodded. "Yes, open it. But be careful, handle gently."

Puzzled, she sat on the nearest chair and opened the loosely closed lid. Dark brown eyes looked up at her. "A puppy." She reached in and lifted the small golden-haired dog into her lap. "You're beautiful."

"She's a golden retriever. Her fur reminds me of the color of your hair." Jackson knelt in front of Samantha as she hugged the pup. "Is it all right? I know you've missed Sergeant since he died of old age almost two years ago. You swore you'd never have another dog. But I saw this one at a friend's house recently." He petted the puppy's fur. "Their dog had four puppies, and this was the runt of the litter. I thought of you, so I asked to buy her."

Samantha rubbed her cheek over the silky fur. "She's precious. Sergeant was just a mutt, but I loved him anyway. He was a great thirteenth birthday present." She put the puppy on the floor and stood. The puppy immediately began to sniff their feet and the furniture. "What shall I call her?"

"You decide. She's yours."

Samantha looked at Jackson. "Thank you."

He reached for her and pulled her close. "Now you can do better than that." He gave her his half smile that always made her body tingle.

She put her arms around his neck and stretched up on her tiptoes to brush her lips across his. Jackson's arms pulled her tight as his mouth ravished hers. His hard cock pushed against her abdomen. The sound of the screen door opening broke them apart.

"Well, well. Finally, I get to see some passion between you two. I was beginning to worry that you'd concocted this whole thing only to meet my demands. I know how persuasive my granddaughter can be. I was sure she'd convinced you to go along with her," Gramps said. He had stepped just inside the door and wore a wide grin. He looked more relaxed then she'd seen him in a long time. A rush of guilt went through her hearing his words.

"What do we have here?" Gramps had knelt down to look at the puppy. Feeling frisky, the small pup ran to Gramps and licked his chin. Gramps picked her up, chuckling.

"I brought her to Samantha as a surprise," Jackson said.

"I'm glad. I've missed having a dog around here. Of course, I guess she'll go with Samantha when she moves to your place."

"I'll bring her around every day, Gramps. I promise."

Gramps shook Jackson's hand. "Good to see you back. Why not join us for dinner? Maria always has enough for company."

"I'd like that. First though, do Samantha and I have time to take a walk? I need to discuss something with her."

"Sure." Gramps glanced at his watch. "We won't eat for another hour. I have to get cleaned up." He glanced down at the puppy, who was trying to chew on his boot. "She'll be safe here. Nothing much she can hurt in this room. I'll ask Maria to keep an eye on her. Go on." He made a motion with his hands for them to leave.

Jackson grabbed Samantha's hand and led her outside. The sunset in the west shed streaks of purple, pink, and yellow across the sky, and a soft, cool breeze blew across Samantha's face. Jackson led her away from the house toward a grove of trees. He didn't stop walking until the house was out of sight.

Samantha tugged at his hand. "What is so important, Jackson? Slow down. I'm almost out of breath."

"This." Jackson swung her around and against a large oak tree. He moved his body hard against hers and cradled her face in his hands. "I've missed you and this." His lips closed on her mouth. She opened her lips, and his tongue invaded, moving along the inside and over her teeth. Involuntarily, her fingers ran through his silky hair as she kissed him back.

He nudged her legs apart and put his full erection against her softness. She moved herself against the ridge, creating a deep ache inside her. His fingers ran along the edge of her short shorts and then underneath to touch the wetness gushing from between her pussy lips.

"You're so hot and slick. You want me as much as I want you. Come home with me tonight."

"I can't. Maria and Gramps will know what we're doing."

He leaned his head back. "Honey, it's natural. See how suspicious your grandfather was because he hadn't seen us show this excitement for each other. Anyway, we have a good excuse. We need to plan for my guests who will arrive tomorrow afternoon and leave Sunday morning. Then, the next Saturday we get married."

"We really shou—"

He stopped her. "We're not going to postpone the wedding. I don't care if we only have my parents, your grandfather, and Maria here."

She leaned her head against his chest and tried to ignore the movement of his fingers sending shivers up her spine. "Janice is coming tomorrow to help."

He gave her a quick peck and stepped back from her. "If I don't stop now, I won't be able to, and we're a little exposed here. We'll continue this at my house, tonight." Taking her hand, he started back. "You can call Janice and see if she wants to fly in with the other guests. The plane will land them on my private airstrip."

"All right." She pushed her hair back and straightened her clothes as they came out of the trees. "Behave at dinner."

Jackson laughed. "It'll be a strain, but I'll do my best."

Samantha ran upstairs to freshen up and then joined Jackson and Gramps at the dinner table. Gramps was in a good mood. He and Jackson talked about the two ranches, while Samantha enjoyed just watching their faces and listening to them. When Jackson mentioned Samantha going to his house for the evening Gramps readily agreed. "I'm tired and going to bed early anyway."

"You don't need to work so hard, Gramps. We have plenty of help, and I can ride out and check on things."

"Don't take my work away from me, child. What would I do with myself but sit around here and miss your grandmother? No, I'll be fine by tomorrow morning. I'll come in earlier in the afternoon."

Although Samantha worried, she knew any further conversation would only upset him and not accomplish anything. She kissed him on the cheek and stuck her head in the kitchen door to tell Maria good-bye. Then, she and Jackson went to Gramps' truck.

"Since you have to drive me home, and you'll be returning on your own, I won't keep you with me as late as usual," Jackson said.

"Like there is anyone around here that would harm me."

"Even in the country, strangers can be passing through."

"I suppose." She climbed into the driver's seat.

Open truck windows let in the sweet fragrance of night-blooming jasmine. Samantha glanced at Jackson. "You look tired."

"I had a busy day, and there's a full weekend ahead."

"Why did you decide to have your employees here at this time? It seems like later after our wedding might have been better."

"Well, there's something I haven't told you. Guess now is as good as any time. You mustn't tell anyone, preferably not even your grandfather or Maria. I trust them, but just a slip and the wrong person might overhear and upset my plans."

Samantha drove into his yard and stopped the truck by the front door. The house was dark, and only the stars and moon lit the area around them. She turned in the seat to face Jackson.

"Whatever are you talking about? You're making it sound very mysterious."

"I'd planned to have it as a wedding surprise for you." Looking directly at her, he said, "About six months ago, I realized the times I was the happiest were when I stayed at the ranch. Building my business had been exciting the first years. Not so much anymore. I'm tired of traveling, staying in hotel rooms, and even when I was at my townhouse or the beach house in Florida, neither felt like home. Not like the ranch did. To shorten the story, I'm turning over my company to one of my senior associates to take on the job as CEO. I'll stay on the board and keep the majority shares." He opened his door. "Let's go inside to discuss this further."

Shocked by his words, Samantha followed him. She'd never expected he'd ever decide to leave the high life in the city. He'd never given any indication he didn't love the traveling and being so busy.

Jackson flipped on lights as he went through to the kitchen. "I'll get us a glass of wine. Make yourself comfortable."

She wandered across the large living room to the side windows. Outside, the trees waved in the breeze and a lone hound dog howled. She wasn't sure how what Jackson had just told her might affect them. She'd expected, wanted to take charge of the ranches, and thought they'd see each other mostly on weekends or maybe not even that often.

"Here's your Riesling wine. Come, join me on the couch. Tell me what you're thinking about?" Jackson asked as she settled at one end of the long sofa and curled her legs under her.

She stared into her wine and then took a sip before speaking. "You let me believe I'd have the running of the ranches while you jetted around doing your corporate business."

"You made the suggestion to run my ranch and yours. I never said yes or no."

Temper rising, she took another big swallow of wine, hoping she'd cool off enough not to lose her temper. "That's semantics. You let me think you agreed."

"No, as usual, when you want your way, you don't look or notice the other person's reaction. You assume they agree with you if they don't verbally say no. So I suppose, knowing you, I am at fault." A wry smile crossed his face.

Samantha handed her empty glass to him. "Now you're being patronizing. I'm going home."

She started to leave. She stopped, surprised to see Jackson's face flush and his lips tighten. He rarely lost his cool.

"Just remember, not a word to anyone. Hopefully, you can get past your childish temper tantrum and help with my guests, perhaps even be my hostess during the activities. They'll arrive at the airport in the morning."

Hot anger rushed through every muscle in her body. She strode quickly to the door and swung it open. "Good night." She slammed the door and hurried to her truck.

"Childish tantrum," she mumbled to herself. How dare he accuse her of having a tantrum. Snapping the truck in gear, she threw dirt from under her wheels and roared off.

* * * *

Jackson watched her leave. He ran a hand through his hair. He must be tired. He'd shown little finesse in that conversation. At least Samantha knew there'd be no rolling over him with her choices. Not all the time. Her control issue was her one major fault. Everyone had at least one. He smiled at the thought. Samantha probably had a handy list she could read to him of his shortcomings.

He had a lot to get done in the next week, if he planned to tie things up in Houston. Plus, he had to convince Samantha to still marry him. Going into the family room, he placed their wineglasses in the sink and headed to his bedroom.

There was one more secret she didn't know. *One that might totally blow them apart, forever.*

Chapter Seven

Samantha drove to the airfield on her own. She'd half expected Jackson to call and apologize. He hadn't. As she drove into the parking area, she saw his truck. Her heart gave a small jolt.

A jet had already landed and parked. A tall, darkly tanned man came down the stairs to the tarmac and waved at Jackson. Their voices carried across the short distance.

"Drake, welcome. I'm glad you rearranged your business to be here this weekend."

"It has taken me much too long to accept your kind invitations. When you said I'd meet the woman who finally convinced my friend to marry, well, then I knew I had to drop everything and meet this incredible woman."

Both men laughed and shook hands. When they turned in her direction, she knew Jackson had seen her. Her curiosity was aroused about this stranger. She glanced at her black slacks and emerald blouse. She was glad she'd decided to dress up a bit for the company.

Jackson led the stranger to her side. "This, my friend, is my bride-to-be, Samantha Riley. Samantha, my best friend from my college years and one of the best international attorneys in the country, Drake Terrell."

"I am pleased to make your acquaintance, Miss Riley. Please ignore the over-glorified description of my job. Jackson tends to exaggerate." He bowed his head to her. "I see how you won my friend's heart. She is beautiful, Jackson."

Samantha blushed. Jackson put his arm around her. "Both inside and out, although a little feisty at times." Jackson tightened his arm when she started to pull away. "I think the other plane is about to land with the rest of our guests."

The three of them watched as the plane landed and taxied closer. Drake's private jet had already started toward a nearby hangar. The plane rolled to a stop, and the door opened. Adults and children hurried down the steps to be greeted by Jackson and introduced to Samantha.

Janice was the last to appear at the top of the plane's stairway. She waited while several families in front of her climbed down.

"Magnificent," Drake said.

Standing close by, Samantha overheard his comment. She glanced his way and noticed his attention was on the door to the plane, where Janice stood. Sunlight sparkled off her auburn hair. The breeze molded her bronze blouse and short skirt against her body and exposed her long, tanned legs.

"Who is she?" Drake asked.

"My best friend, Janice Dedrick. She's an attorney in Houston. You've never met her at some of your lawyer gatherings?"

"No. I'm seldom in Houston. Mainly I go there to visit Jackson when he needs help with any international legal concerns." He smiled at Samantha. "I find I'm even more pleased to have made this trip."

Samantha studied his hawk-like features. "You will remember she is dear to me."

Dark, mysterious eyes looked deep into hers. He nodded his head. "I will."

Jackson had arranged for the children to have a hayride back to the ranch. There was much giggling and rowdy laughter before they all settled down, and the wagon, pulled by two horses, began to slowly head along a dirt path that led directly to the barn. Two parents had climbed on board to chaperone the excited children. Samantha smiled at the group as they left.

"In a few years we can start taking our children on hayrides," Jackson whispered in her ear. A shiver brushed over her.

She started to reply when Janice, hurrying across the tarmac, came to her side. "You two look cozy," she teased.

"I'm so glad you're here." Samantha hugged her friend tight. "At least I know one person in this crowd."

"Actually, you know at least two," Drake Terrell said as he joined them. "Won't you introduce me to this lovely lady?"

"I'm not sure I should, but Janice can take care of herself. Janice, this is Drake Terrell, Jackson's best friend from college. He's an international attorney. Drake, my best friend, Janice Dedrick."

"I've heard of you, Mr. Terrell. You are being modest if you're saying you are just an international attorney. If I'm not mistaken, you also do sensitive negotiations for our country and its allies."

"Few people are aware of my other commitments. I'd rather it stay that way."

Samantha saw the change in his face. His hawk-like features were more defined, and his eyes no longer looked mysterious. They made her shiver. He would be a dangerous man to cross.

Janice didn't smile. "I apologize." She glanced around. "No one is close enough to have heard. I was told about you in strictest confidence. I'm sure Samantha won't tell anyone."

"Let's head to my ranch, Janice." Samantha saw Jackson herding the adults into several large cars and some of the men into trucks. "Everything seems to be in control here. We have a lot to discuss to plan my wedding. If you'll excuse us, Drake?"

He nodded his head and stepped back. But Samantha felt his hard stare all the way to the car and was sure Janice did, too.

* * * *

Samantha watched as Janice unpacked her bag in the guest room. She didn't miss the slight tremble in her friend's hands.

"He upset you."

"Who?"

"Janice, we've known each other too long for you to pretend. Drake Terrell upset my unflappable friend. I must admit he strikes me as dangerous."

"He didn't scare me."

"Then what? You haven't given a man a second thought since your fiancé died in that car crash a month before your wedding."

"That was four years ago."

"I know. So?"

"He's too good looking, too sure of himself, just too much."

"Watch out, my friend, that sounds a lot like attraction."

"Let me change and then we'll ride to the place you're talking about having your wedding."

"Changing the subject. All right. I'm going to check with Jackson and see if he needs any help. Meet you at the barn in thirty minutes."

Samantha slipped into Gramps' office for privacy. He'd ridden out with his foreman earlier. Jackson's phone rang several times before a woman answered.

"Stone's residence. May I help you?"

"I'd like to speak with Jackson."

"Who's calling?"

"Samantha Riley."

"Oh, Miss Riley, I'm sorry I didn't recognize your voice. This is Anna Murphy. I came down to help Mr. Stone with all his guests. You just missed him. He and most of the others went horseback riding. The children are here playing games under the supervision of several nannies he hired for the weekend."

"He certainly has all the activities well planned."

"Shall I tell him you called?"

"Yes, Mrs. Murphy. Thank you."

"Please call me Anna. Nice talking with you."

Samantha hung up the phone. *He could have asked if Janice and I wanted to go riding. But, I guess we did leave rather abruptly. He and I really haven't resolved our disagreement from the other night.* She shrugged her shoulders and stretched. Glancing at her watch, she decided it was time to head to the barn and pick out a horse for Janice.

When she stepped inside the shadowy interior, a small furry ball scampered to her feet. She knelt and picked up the bundle of energy. "I must decide on a name for you." The pup barked as though in agreement. Ever since the puppy wet the carpet, Maria had sent her to the barn until she was trained not to ruin the furniture and floors. Samantha had been so busy that one of the older ranch hands had offered to work with the pup.

"Who's that?" Janice asked. She walked up beside Samantha.

"Jackson brought her back from Houston as a surprise for me. I can't seem to think of an appropriate name."

Janice reached out to take the puppy from Samantha and laughed when the small pup licked her face. "The only name that fits is Sunshine. Even in this dark barn, her golden coat glows."

"You can put her down. She won't run away. I thought you might like this gray mare, Tilley. She's older and very gentle."

"Good. Horses are scary. They're so tall, and I'm so far from the ground when I'm on their back. I never ride except when I visit you and you insist. Let's get this over with."

"We can go by truck."

"Then what are we waiting for?" Janice brightened. "I'm anxious to see this special place."

Samantha led the way through the barn to the back where the old truck had been parked. "I slipped my keys in my pocket just in case." She swung into the driver's side. "Hold on. The road is bumpy."

"Why am I not surprised?" Janice mumbled.

About three miles out, Janice relaxed in her seat. "This isn't bad."

"You spoke too soon." Samantha turned the wheel to the right, and the lane narrowed to two ruts and the bumps began. By the time they rode several miles, Janice held the side of the door in a tight grip.

"Are we close?"

"Almost there."

"What's so special about this place?"

"Wait. I want to see your initial reaction."

Samantha slowed and parked on the right of the narrow drive.

"We'll walk from here."

She and Janice strolled along the rutted pathway and turned left to a wider opening, not exactly a road but more a trail. The trees were thicker in this area, and ahead Samantha saw what, in her mind, she called her wedding cathedral. A long line of tall trees created a canopy over the trail, and at the end was a hill where a small waterfall flowed gently into the creek below. Sunlight sparkled off the silver water, and the sounds of the falls created their own music.

Secretly, Samantha had dreamed of being married in this spot, early in the morning as the sun rose and flooded the area with light. She glanced at Janice and saw a reflection of how she must have looked the first time her grandmother brought her here.

"A natural sacred place," her grandma said. She had spoken in hushed tones. "Around the world I believe there are places like this fashioned by nature to remind man of his deep attachment to all things."

Janice had tears in her eyes when she faced Samantha. "It is the most perfect spot for a wedding."

"I think so." Samantha sat on the grassy area by the creek. Janice joined her. Each quiet, caught up in their own thoughts.

Finally, Samantha took a deep breath. "Let's head back. There are plans to make and places to go," she said, smiling across at her friend.

They'd just gotten to the truck when Samantha heard a horse snort. She glanced around and saw Jackson riding his mare across the dusty path to the right of them. "Jackson, where is your company?"

"My foreman is taking them to the ranch for a light lunch and rest. We'll gather in the family room for cocktails at six. Until then I have a few free hours. We need to talk."

"I've got to take Janice back."

"How about Janice drives herself back, and you get up here with me?"

"I can't desert her out here in the wilderness."

"Really, Sam. I'm quite grown up. I'm sure I can find my way back to the ranch house. It was only one turn." Janice must have seen her hesitation. "Go. I'll be fine."

Jackson leaned down. "Take my hand. Put your foot on my boot, and I'll pull you up in front of me."

Samantha glanced from her friend to him. "All right. If you get lost, Janice, it's your own fault." She put her hand in Jackson's. He quickly pulled her into his arms.

They waited a minute to see Janice get the truck turned around and headed back. Jackson tightened his arm around Samantha's waist. He leaned forward and whispered in her ear. "Now I have you all to myself."

She caught her breath as sharp desire shot straight down her body. "Where are we going?"

"All the men are working on the fence along the west section. Your grandfather stopped by on his way to that same area. We'll go east where we can be sure of privacy."

Samantha leaned back in his embrace as they rode along. His wide chest and strong arms encircled her. She drew in a deep breath. His spicy, earthy male fragrance filled her lungs. They rode across a vast field covered with pink, white, and blue wildflowers waving in the breeze. Her earlier sense of peace held her in its cocoon.

"How much farther?" she asked.

"Just around this bend. You remember this place."

Samantha glanced around at him. "We used to picnic here years ago."

"Anna packed us a lunch. I've got the food in my saddlebag. There's our spot." He nodded toward a small grove of trees. The creek, which ran through the ranch, gurgled over rocks, and circled around one side of the oaks. They rode toward the shade. Jackson helped Samantha down and then tied his horse to a tree, close enough to the stream for his stallion to take a drink.

Samantha unpacked the food and several bottles of water. She spread out the blanket and opened several small containers holding sliced chicken, chips, and fruit.

"Looks good." She sat waiting for Jackson. His horse had drunk some water and now chewed on an apple he'd given him.

Jackson strolled across to Samantha. "This is a pleasant place to eat and discuss our misunderstanding the other night." He sat down across from her.

"You were right. I ought to have told you, but it's so important that no word get out until I've decided who will replace me. No one has any idea of my plans except Drake, Mrs. Haverty, and a couple of CEOs of companies I do business with overseas."

"Who will replace you?"

He smiled at her. "I'm hoping you'll help me decide. The main reason I'm having this weekend get-together is to see the man and woman I'm considering under informal circumstances. I want to see their interaction with the others and their families."

She nodded. "That's a good idea."

He lay back and put his hands behind his head, staring up at the clear blue sky. "I'm not totally sure why my giving up the business upset you. I'd hoped you might be pleased."

"When I asked you to marry me, I pictured you traveling with your business and only coming home occasionally. I'd be busy with the two ranches. We'd have a modern, sensible marriage without all the turmoil."

He turned toward her. "By turmoil, I assume you mean sex."

"Well, yes." She felt her face redden. He grinned at her with the sexy smile that always made her ache for his touch.

"And after being in *turmoil* with me a time or two, do you still feel that way?"

Not ready to admit that her feelings might be different, she quickly changed the subject. "Sit up and eat. Anna fixed this great lunch for us." Even to her, her voice sounded tight and husky.

Jackson did as she said and faced her. "Feed me. I'll have the chicken first."

She started to protest but saw the lust shining in his eyes. Without a thought, she found her hand taking a piece of chicken and placing it in his mouth. He nipped at her fingers before she moved away.

"Good."

Next she handed him a purple grape. This time he took hold of her hand and licked her finger. Fire traveled her nerve endings straight to her core. He reached for a peach and held it to her lips. She bit through the skin. The sweet juice ran down her chin.

He leaned forward and licked her lips, her chin, and neck. "Best peach I ever tasted."

"Stop this, Jackson. We're out in the open. Behave."

Glancing around, he shook his head no. "We're in the shade of a tree with several other trees around us. Hardly right in the open."

"Nevertheless—" Before she said another word, Jackson had shoved the food to the side, pushed her down on the blanket, and straddled her.

"What are you doing? Get off."

He leaned close to her face and took a deep breath. "You always smell tantalizing." He kissed the shell of her ear and nuzzled her cheek. "I'll stop if you really want me to."

When she opened her mouth to say yes, he covered her lips, his tongue delving deep into the soft recesses of her mouth. Large, warm hands cupped her face. Her heartbeat sped up at his touch.

He pulled back. "Still want me to stop?"

"You don't play fair."

Jackson chuckled. "Not when I want something badly."

His hands moved to her blouse and began to unbutton it.

"Stop." She placed her hands on his. "I am not making love in the open where anybody can ride by."

"There isn't a person in ten miles. Wait." He took quick strides to his horse and reached into the other saddle bag. He came back carrying a large towel. "If in the remote possibility a person comes by, I'll throw this towel over you. I brought towels in case we wanted to take a dip in the stream."

"You planned this all along."

"Of course." He tickled her neck with his breath and light kisses. She scrunched her neck and pulled away laughing.

"This is thirsty work." Jackson opened a bottle of water, took a sip then poured a stream of the cool liquid on her chest between the opening of her blouse.

"That's cold," she said as she instinctively raised her upper body.

He pushed her back down. "Stay." He quickly removed her boots, and her shirt and bra, pushing them aside so he could sip what water was left from between her breasts. The cool was instantly replaced by hot desire. His tongue licked around each breast and sucked on her tight nipples. His mouth followed his hands as he moved further along her body. He unfastened her buckle, her button on her jeans, and pulled the zipper down. Before she thought to stop him, he yanked all her clothing from the waist down off.

"Beautiful." He kneeled at her feet in admiration. She tried to cover herself with her hands. He pushed them aside. "No one can see you, but me. If there was a crowd out there, they'd be yelling and cheering us on. Relax, honey. Look around. Breathe in the fresh air."

Samantha lay still. Sunlight shone in between the leaves of the tree above. A cool breeze rippled across her sensitive skin. Shade from the large branches cast shadows across her body. She hated to admit there was a sense of freedom lying here open to the world.

Jackson leaned over her. She watched as his fingers separated her lower lips and his mouth descended over her clit.

His lips brushed along her clit, tasting, caressing, gentle as a butterfly's touch.

Her arms and legs were sinking into the soft ground. Her blood turned to warm honey as he seduced every inch of her body. His mouth pressed more urgently, and his tongue swirled around her clit. He reached for her breasts with his hands, and his thumb and forefinger rolled her tight nipples between them.

Her body arched. She moaned and looked upward. The vast openness fueled her desire, sending her spiraling out of control. A wave of pleasure surged from her feet over her body as he lapped up her wetness. Her strongest orgasm ever flooded through her.

* * * *

Jackson raised his head and watched as her body arched and trembled. He bent and kissed her then moved to her side. Sitting up, he wiped his mouth on the towel. He took a long swallow of water. After he put the bottle down, he lay beside her.

"Now, help me out of my shirt and jeans then straddle me."

Samantha unbuttoned his shirt, leaving it open but not completely off. She struggled with his large belt buckle but got it unhooked, unfastened his jeans, and moved to his feet where she tugged his boots off and then his jeans. He lay silently watching her every movement. Each touch of her hands sent heat sizzling along his lower body. When she had him nude, she put her leg over him and settled herself across the top of his thighs. Her fingers brushed across his chest and his nipples. His voracious appetite for her went soaring out of sight. He couldn't not touch her.

Her breasts were heavy and soft when he cupped his hands around them. Her nipples pebbled. Moving upward, she rubbed herself across his aching dick, then arched her back and stared at the sky while her body trembled in response. Her long golden hair fell down her naked back, and his cock jerked, impatient to be deep inside her hot pussy. She looked like a golden goddess sitting above him. He wanted to bury himself to his balls inside her wet, tight heat.

He reached for his jeans where she'd thrown them beside him and took a condom out of his back pocket. "Open it, cover me, and put me inside your hot pussy." If his erotic words shocked her, she hid it well. He wanted her so desperately, he'd probably stick his thumb through the condom if he tried to put it on himself.

Her small, soft hands positioned him and rolled the condom along the length of his throbbing cock. She stared into his eyes as she sat firmly, taking him smoothly inside her in one long stroke. Pulsing heat grabbed him. When she wiggled, his temperature rose straight to boiling. She licked his nipples as she began to move slowly up and down. Leaning across his chest, she nibbled at the edge of his jaw. He forced himself to lay still and let her mouth and fingers explore his body.

Suddenly, her one hand moved to cup his sac.

"Damn, that feels good," he managed to grit out through clenched teeth. Grasping her hips, he moved her up and down, again against his hard cock, and a rush of electricity shot straight up his spine, sending shock waves spreading across his body. He held her hard against him as the wave of pleasure, almost pain it was so intense, rolled over every inch of his skin.

Seeing her begin to shudder, a look of joy on her face, intensified his pleasure, and he held her hard against him until she collapsed on his chest. Their pounding hearts beat against each other.

When her breathing had slowed, Samantha moved her leg over him and stood. She brushed her hair off her neck. Sunlight sent a glow to her skin and brightened the already golden color of her hair. She'd never looked as magnificent, and he'd never loved her more.

She reached for his saddlebag and retrieved another bottle of water. After taking several sips, she handed the bottle to him. He sat up and pulled her close to his side while he drank. His hand curved around her waist, his fingers brushing the underside of her breast.

* * * *

She hadn't expected to ever be naked outdoors, much less make love. For this one glorious moment, she didn't care. She relished the touch of the breeze and the warmth of the sun on her skin, and the hot, lustful look in Jackson's eyes only increased her own desire. What was happening to her? Even after all this she wanted him more, now.

He must have read the message in her face and body because he pulled her down and flipped her under him.

"Do you care about the damn condom?" he asked as he ripped the old one off. "I want to feel closer to you."

"Go ahead." They'd be married in seven days, and she was on birth control anyway. A wicked wildness washed over her. She spread her legs and threw her arms open.

Jackson, already hard, surged into her. His mouth ravished hers, and he took her hard and fast again. The tide of pleasure grabbed them both at the same time and left them shaking in each other's arms.

Chapter Eight

Samantha had been relaxed all afternoon. Janice had teased her about the distant look in her eyes. Now, dressed and ready for Jackson's cocktail party, she glanced at herself in the mirror.

Her strapless black dress fell loose to just above her knees. She added the diamond earrings and necklace Jackson had given her. High-heeled patent sandals and a matching purse completed her outfit. Janice had arranged her golden hair in a twist with long curls brushing the nape of her neck.

"Every man at the party is going to envy Jackson tonight," Janice said as she came back into the room. "It's time we left. Jackson sent a car for us."

"You look very good yourself," Samantha said. "That color of emerald green is stunning on you. Are you dressing for anyone in particular?"

"Nope. Not dressing for anyone but myself."

"Liar," Samantha whispered. She followed Janice down the stairs.

Gramps spoke to them from the door of his study. "Two beautiful women." He smiled at Janice and kissed Samantha's cheek. "Have fun."

They waved and hurried out to the long limousine waiting to whisk them to the party. They'd barely gotten settled before the chauffeur was opening the car door at Jackson's. Lights shown from all the front windows. They rang the doorbell, and Anna came to the door.

"Welcome, Miss Riley. Mr. Stone is out on the terrace with some of the guests, and the rest are in the family room."

"Mrs. Murphy, this is my friend, Janice Dedrick. We'll join the group in the family room."

Mrs. Murphy smiled at Janice. "Pleased to meet you. I'm sure I'll see you again. I'm Mr. Stone's housekeeper and cook."

She waved them in and hurried back to the kitchen. Samantha and Janice strolled around the living room and into the crowded adjoining room.

"I like his house," Janice said.

"Miss Riley, it's nice to see you again." Mr. Greenlee came forward with a small, dark-haired woman at his side and two small boys following them. "This is my wife, Beth, and my sons, Charles, who is six, and Frank, who is four. Beth, Miss Riley is engaged to Mr. Stone."

"You're a lucky lady. He's a very nice man and has been good to my husband and me. When I was diagnosed with breast cancer three years ago, he made sure I saw the best specialist and gave my husband time off to be with me and the boys. I told Charlie that he'd better work extra hard to pay him back."

Mr. Greenlee blushed but added, "He is the best boss I've had."

"Thank you for telling me. I've known Jackson since I moved here at ten years old. He's always been good to me, too."

"Ah," Mrs. Greenlee said. "Most everyone thought this was so sudden, but none of us realized you'd known each other that long. How romantic."

"Beth, we better move on. Miss Riley hasn't had time to get a drink, and I'm sure others want to meet her."

Samantha watched them blend back into a group standing near the open door to the patio and pool. Glancing around, she realized Janice had slipped away. She'd get a drink and find her.

"You really think this marriage will work." Lunette walked up behind her. "It may take me a while to convince him he's made a mistake, but he will come to that realization." Her eyes shot darts of anger at Samantha. "Don't underestimate what I will do, to have whatever it is I want."

"Excuse me, Lunette. I'm going to get a glass of wine." She deliberately walked in the opposite direction from the woman and her cloying perfume.

Samantha felt the heat of Lunette's glare burning between her shoulder blades. She forced herself to show no reaction. There wasn't anything the woman could do but talk, and she suspected most people would disregard what she said as the ranting of a jealous woman.

A waiter came by carrying a tray of white wine. Samantha took a glass and headed outside. She spotted Jackson's head in a group of men standing by the far end of the pool. To the right was the large lounge chair where she and Jackson had made love under the night sky. Her face warmed at the memory. To take her mind off those thoughts, she looked for Janice.

Janice stood in a shadowy corner with Drake. He towered over her friend and appeared to be conversing seriously about something. Janice shook her head, stepped around him, and walked toward the lighted area. Samantha waved, and Janice headed toward her.

She grabbed a glass of red wine from a waiter's tray and handed it to Janice. "What's wrong? You look upset."

"That man is the most egotistical, arrogant—well, I won't go over all the superlatives to describe him. He's annoying and makes me angry quicker than anyone I've known."

"I don't think I've ever seen you really angry."

Janice stopped a waiter and took a small plate of roasted oysters and grilled mushrooms off his tray. "Let's sit here." She pointed to a round table right behind them. "We'll eat some appetizers and maybe feel better."

They stepped back to the table. Samantha grabbed a plate of cheese and apple slices and joined Janice. The delicious fragrance of roast beef came from the kitchen area. "Jackson is busy socializing. His cook obviously has everything under control so we get to relax and talk. The rest of the weekend will be full. He's planning a huge barbecue tomorrow. His staff is doing a wonderful job, which frees me from having to do much."

"You can be lazy tonight, but we still have your invitations to send out, and we have to complete all the plans for your wedding before next weekend," Janice reminded her.

"Keep her at it, Janice," Jackson said as he leaned down and brushed a kiss across Samantha's cheek. "Are you two enjoying yourselves?"

"It's lovely, Jackson," Janice said.

"Mind if I take Samantha away for a few minutes?"

"Not at all. I'm going to sit here and enjoy the sunset." Janice smiled as Jackson pulled out Samantha's chair and put his arm around her waist.

"I'll see you inside shortly," Samantha said.

Jackson pulled her closer and whispered in her ear. "Let's walk around the side and go down to the barn. I want to ask you to do me a favor."

She looked at him, puzzled by his words. "You had most of the afternoon to ask me."

"True." He smiled. "But my attention got diverted to other matters."

They slipped out a side door and walked briskly across the yard to the stable. Inside, except for a dim bulb in the back, the area was dark and smelled of horses and hay. A pleasant odor to Samantha.

Jackson turned her toward him and kissed her forehead. Samantha stepped out of his arms.

"If we get started, you'll forget to ask me your favor."

"Sad, but true. I'd like you to watch my associates and their families tonight and tomorrow during activities. Next week I'll be making my decision. I'd like your input."

His words pleased her. "I wasn't sure you were serious about wanting my opinion," she said.

"Why not?" He hugged her close again. "I've always considered you observant and smart about people, except for your poor choices in male friends. That is except for me of course. I have three senior associates. You've met two. I'll introduce Paul Thomas to you tonight, although he's too close to retirement. I'm really considering either Charles or Lunette."

Samantha hesitated. She already knew where her vote would go. "I think you should ask someone else for input."

Jackson leaned back, trying to see her expression. "Really? Why?"

"It's a woman thing. She irritates me. I'm sure it's mutual. My vote would definitely go for Mr. Greenlee. I liked his family a lot. They'll keep him grounded."

"Interesting. Has Lunette said something to upset you?"

"Let's just leave it with what I said. We'd better go back. I'm sure the efficient Mrs. Murphy has dinner on the table."

Jackson started to speak, but instead he put his arm through hers, and they strolled back through the dark to the lighted house.

The dinner went well. All the guests chatted happily, and the food was delicious. When Samantha thought enough time had passed, she found Jackson to tell him good night.

"I'm tired. Tomorrow will be another busy day."

He pulled her outside and wrapped his arms around her. "I'm going back with Drake Sunday. There's a lot to be done before I can pick a CEO and resign. I want it finished before our wedding."

Samantha leaned her head into his chest. She breathed in his scent. Her lips kissed his chest where his shirt was unbuttoned. He pulled her tighter, and she felt his arousal.

Lifting her head, she smiled. "You'll miss me?"

"I will, but after next Saturday, I'll have you completely to myself and at my mercy." His husky voice sent a shiver of desire down her spine.

"Janice is staying the week. She'll help get everything set for the wedding. She's the most organized person I know." Samantha pulled back. "Got to go. See you tomorrow." She waved before hurrying into the house to find her friend and escape to the quiet of Gramps' ranch.

"I was ready to go," Janice said when they were climbing into the limo. "And I'll be ready as you are to see them fly away."

"Them? Or him?"

"Samantha, what is it with you? I've told you I'm not interested in the man."

"Ah, but you knew who I was talking about."

Janice snuggled down in her seat. "Hush, I'm sleepy."

* * * *

"This is a mad house," Samantha said. Children ran around the yard, yelling and laughing. Their parents strolled around the house and barn sipping on tall, cool drinks.

Samantha and Janice joined Jackson at one of the barbecue pits.

"After last night, I thought I'd never be hungry again, but that seductive fragrance has my mouth watering," Samantha said.

Jackson pulled a piece of rib meat from the bone and proceeded to feed her. "Good?"

"Hmm, yes." She licked his finger just before he pulled it back. She glanced around. Janice had joined some women a few feet to the left. Samantha leaned close. "I think I'll cover you in barbecue sauce," she whispered to Jackson, "and lick it off."

His eyes blazed then went very dark. "Keep tempting me and I'll carry you away right now."

Samantha wasn't sure if he was teasing her or not but chose to change the subject. "You'll be leaving early tomorrow?"

He nodded. "I'll call during the week, just so you don't forget who you're marrying."

"Funny."

"I try. After I decide on a CEO and tell them, I'll let you know how it went."

Samantha glanced around. Mr. Greenlee's boys were standing in line with the other children for a ride on a pony. Mr. Greenlee and his wife stood nearby looking relaxed and happy.

She continued to search the crowd until she spotted Lunette leaning close to Drake while they talked. Today she had dressed in skintight jeans and a loose blouse that still emphasized her full breasts.

"You really don't like her."

"Who?" Samantha asked, turning back to Jackson.

"Forget her, let's go for a hayride," he said. Pulling Samantha to his side, he walked with her in the opposite direction from Drake and Lunette.

Samantha spotted Janice leaning against a shade tree. Her attention obviously centered on Drake. A frown wrinkled her forehead.

"Janice," she called out. Janice turned and quickly put a smile on her face. "Join us," Samantha said. "We're going on a hayride."

"Sure." Janice took one last glance behind her before walking to the wagon filled with hay.

Children clamored to join the adults. Soon little and big kids swarmed around them and on them. Jackson had pulled Samantha down beside him on top of a large pile of hay.

Samantha leaned in close. "Sure you still want children?"

"At least four." He laughed at her shocked expression. The wagon jerked as they started off. A small hand tugged at Jackson's arm.

"I'm scared." Blonde hair fell around her tiny face, and tears ran out of large blue eyes.

Jackson picked her up and placed her between him and Samantha. "Is that better?"

The little girl hiccupped and nodded her head yes. She gave Jackson a big smile.

"I think she just wrapped you around her little finger," Samantha quipped. She looked over the child's head and stared into Jackson's smiling eyes. Her heart lurched. *What in the world have I done?* She couldn't deny her feelings any longer. *I've fallen in love with Jackson.*

The rest of the party went by in a haze. All of her denial had been false. Stunned by her realization, she found herself watching Jackson all afternoon. She noted how easy it was for him to move from one group to the next. It was obvious he was well-liked. She admired his ability to talk with everyone, including the children.

Loving him frightened her. She'd wanted a sensible marriage with her here running the ranch and him taking care of his business. Her world had turned upside down. She didn't want to love him. *Everyone I love dies.* The thought seared across her brain. Where did that come from? How ridiculous.

"Sam"—Janice touched her arm—"are you all right?"

"Of course, why do you ask?"

"Well you've been standing in the same spot for the last ten minutes and frowning at that poor horse inside the corral like you'd like to kick him."

Samantha shook herself. "I must be tired. Isn't it time for this party to end?"

Janice looked at Samantha with a worried expression on her face. "I think it's time enough that we can leave. Let's go to the car. I'll drive."

"Sounds wonderful. But, I have to be polite and tell them all good-bye."

"Then I'll walk with you. We'll make it short."

After endless handshaking, a few hugs, and a kiss from Jackson, Samantha climbed into the passenger seat of her car. She closed her eyes. "Thanks, Janice. Did I do the good-byes all right?"

"Don't worry. You fooled everyone but me—and Jackson."

Later that evening, Jackson called. He was concerned about her since she'd left the barbecue early. Samantha appeased him by telling him that something she'd eaten hadn't agreed with her, but the sick feeling had passed.

Janice, being in the same room when Samantha answered the call, gave her a wry smile when she hung up. "You might fool him with that story. Not me."

They'd dressed in their pajamas and sat curled into soft leather chairs in the family room. The muted TV flashed the only light in the room. Gramps had retired much earlier.

Taking a handful of popcorn from the bowl on the table between them, Samantha faced Janice.

"I love Jackson."

"Well, I hope so. You are marrying him next Saturday."

"This wasn't supposed to happen. I wanted a convenient, sensible marriage."

"Why? I'd think loving your husband would be much more preferable."

"I don't know. I had the weirdest thought just before you rescued me and took me home."

Janice didn't speak. She waited patiently.

"It was that I didn't want to love anyone because the people I love die. Isn't that stupid?"

"Not really, it's what I've suspected."

"What?"

"Sam, the few men you've had serious relationships with have been good men. But, you always found some fault in them and ended things." She held her hand up when Samantha started to speak. "Let me finish. I've never had the nerve to say this. If I stop now, I won't.

"The attraction between you and Jackson has been evident for years to others, and yet you took care to run away if he looked like he might respond to you.

"My belief is that the losses in your life have affected you more than you've been willing to admit. You lost your parents at a young age, both suddenly. Your grandmother died of an unexpected heart attack. You took her loss hard."

"Why didn't you suggest this to me before?"

"It was only my supposition. You'd have denied it. You had to make the discovery yourself."

"I said the thought crossed my mind. I didn't say I believed it."

"You do. Quit trying to fool yourself. The man loves you, and you love him. How lucky can you get? Don't let the past ruin your future." Janice stood and stretched. "I'm going to bed. I probably don't know what I'm talking about." She leaned down and kissed the top of Samantha's head. "Tomorrow we start to seriously work on your wedding."

"Good night." Samantha watched as her friend left the room.

Janice's response to what she'd said had not been what she expected or wanted to hear.

What do I do now? I wish I could bury that thought—never think of it again. It was too late. Admitting she loved Jackson had her feeling shaky and exposed.

No, vulnerable and scared.

Chapter Nine

Samantha and Janice had taken a trip to San Antonio. Samantha drove into a parking place behind the house. "I wonder if Gramps is in from the fields. I worry about him. He's been looking more tired lately."

"It's probably just all the excitement about your engagement and upcoming wedding. He seems very happy you're marrying Jackson."

"He let me know how pleased he was the night Jackson came to dinner and asked for my hand." Samantha chuckled. "He was tickled that Jackson asked him. An old-fashioned tradition, but then Gramps would expect it."

"Your Gramps is a sweet man." Janice opened the car door. "I'm glad our trip was successful and didn't take too long. We found you the perfect wedding gown." She climbed out and stretched. "I'm going to shower and change before supper. See you later."

Samantha opened the trunk and took out her dress. She was thrilled with her choice and couldn't wait to see Jackson's expression on their wedding day. It still felt unreal that they would be man and wife in three short days. She went in through the kitchen to show Maria what she'd bought, but no one was around. Gramps' study door stood half open and the room empty. He wasn't home either. Suddenly, a flash of yellow fur came rushing at her. Sunshine jumped up and down at her feet and barked.

"Where did you come from?"

Her grandfather's foreman stuck his head in the door. "She's been missing you folks. I brought her from the barn."

She picked the puppy up, and Sunshine licked her face. Samantha smiled. "Thanks. I think we both need each other." The foreman waved and walked toward the corral.

"I'm leaving you," she said to the puppy. "Just for a moment." Starting to climb the stairs, a let-down feeling washed over her. She was tired and disappointed that Jackson hadn't called the last few days. *I'm being silly. I refuse to mope over not getting a phone call.* Samantha hung her gown in her closet and headed for the shower.

At six, when neither Maria nor Gramps had appeared, Samantha began to worry. She sat in Gramps' study. The scent of his cigar and Old Spice made her lonely. Sunshine had cuddled in her lap.

Gramps and Maria hadn't expected her and Janice back until tomorrow, but since they'd found the dress so quickly they'd cut their trip short. Still, where could they be? Samantha reached for the phone just as it rang. She jerked back then took a breath and answered.

"Sam," Maria said. "I got a call from the foreman that you'd gotten home early. I hope you didn't worry."

"I was beginning to. Where are you and Gramps?"

"Your grandfather gave me the time off while you were gone. He said he planned to visit a friend in Houston. We'll both be returning tomorrow."

"That's strange. I didn't know Gramps had a friend in the big city. Thanks for calling, Maria. See you tomorrow."

Samantha hung up the phone. She'd known Maria long enough to hear the hesitation in her voice. There was something she didn't tell her. Before she moved from the phone, it rang again. No calls for two days and now the calls came one after another.

"Hello," Samantha said.

"Miss me?"

"I haven't had time. I've been busy," she fibbed. Jackson's low, husky tone made her toes curl.

He laughed. "You're annoyed because I haven't called. The past few days have been so hectic. But I've decided on my CEO and made the announcement today."

"Who?"

"Your choice, Mr. Greenlee. He was totally surprised and pleased."

"I imagine Lunette was also surprised and not pleased."

"You're right. She didn't take it well at all. Surprisingly, she thought you had something to do with my not choosing her. I told her I'd made the final decision. I did offer for her to be the head consultant on the overseas accounts. She refused and stalked out of my office. I'm sure she'll get and take an offer from my number one competitor, Scott Perkins."

"Can she hurt the business?" Samantha ran her fingers through Sunshine's fur. The pup laid her head down, about to go to sleep.

"Maybe a little. Not much though. One of the reasons I had several associates was so no one person knew everything. Because of that, I may need to come in for a few weeks after our honeymoon to tie up any loose ends and make sure Greenlee has all his questions answered."

"Where are we going on our honeymoon?"

"You'll be surprised, but, believe me, not disappointed."

"I don't like surprises. I won't know what to pack."

"You only need the dress you wear on the plane and one to return in. I intend to keep you naked most of the time."

Her face flushed hot from the heat his words triggered in her body. Her heartbeat pounded at the thought. "Dream on. I'll pack casual, and if it isn't appropriate, it's your fault."

"I'm going to make you eat those words. Got to go. See you Friday for the rehearsal dinner. Mom and Dad will arrive that afternoon. Bye."

Janice knocked on the study door. "From the heightened color in your face, I'd say you just talked to Jackson."

"And Maria. She and Gramps won't be back until tomorrow. Let's drive into Saddle Creek and get pizza." Samantha took Sunshine and placed her in her bed in the kitchen.

"Sounds good. We'll go over the list of things to do. I think we can check off most everything as done."

"You missed your calling, Janice. You'd have made an excellent wedding planner."

"Go wash your mouth out. That'd be my last choice."

* * * *

The weatherman had promised her wedding day would be sunny and warm. Samantha stood at her bedroom window. The sun hadn't risen yet. They'd planned to have the wedding start just when the sky was beginning to lighten so the sunrise would shine full on them during the ceremony.

Samantha sipped the cup of tea she'd slipped downstairs and made. Yesterday they'd practiced the ceremony and had the dinner at Jackson's house. She'd been happy to see his parents. They'd always been kind to her and were pleased about Jackson and her marrying.

Jackson had been affectionate, but—Samantha smiled—restrained somewhat around his parents and Gramps.

"You're awake." Janice poked her head around the door. "Time to get you dressed."

"I can manage. Go get yourself ready."

"All right. I'm so excited for you."

In a short time, she, Maria, Gramps, and Janice were headed to the place where she'd be married. They'd taken the truck with the windows closed to preserve her hairdo. They had to walk the last part. Samantha had worn jeans, a casual shirt, and sandals until they got to the tent that had been erected to the side and behind the trees. There she'd freshen her makeup and put on her gown. They'd arrived early so no one would see her until she started down the path that had been covered with a thin layer of smooth wood.

Janice peeked out. "Looks like everyone is about here." She laughed. "Including Sunshine, who's getting much attention."

Samantha looked out between the tent flaps. Patio lights had been set up around the walkway to the immediate area, then tall candelabras were positioned along the path to the front where she and Jackson would say their vows. One of the cowhands had made sure the candles were lit. The two violin players were arranging their music.

"The ceremony will start soon," Janice said and pulled Samantha back to check on her appearance one last time.

"It better if we want to be down the aisle before the sun is completely up."

"You look beautiful." Janice smiled at her.

"Thanks, you don't look bad yourself. Who would have thought a redhead could wear pink?"

"It's the shade of pink, and I have auburn hair."

"There's the music, our cue. You first, Janice." Janice nodded and walked out of the tent.

Samantha took a deep breath and stepped onto the wood path. She smiled at Gramps when he walked up to her. "You look very handsome, Gramps."

"I had to put on my best suit to give my best girl to Jackson. It's hard to let you go, but time. I can't wait for all those great-grandbabies."

"Gramps. Give us time. Don't rush us." She kissed his cheek then turned to look at the beautiful scene set out before her. All along the walkway, flowers attached to soft chiffon had been placed at the end of each aisle of chairs. Janice had just arrived at the front where the minister, Jackson, and his father waited.

A breeze rippled through the canopy of trees making a lovely rustling sound. The timing was perfect. As Samantha took her first step, the sun popped up from the horizon flooding the area in light. She heard the murmur amongst her guests of family and close friends. She knew her strapless, cream-colored silk organza gown must be glowing as she'd hoped, especially her beaded satin belt.

She looked at Jackson. His smile warmed her heart. She never remembered those last few steps to his side. She did remember Gramps putting her hand in Jackson's and the glint in Jackson's eyes as he looked at her.

He spoke his vows clearly, his voice amplified by the arrangement of the trees, like a cathedral. The sweet smell of pine scented the air, and the sound from the waterfall was fitting music to complement the ceremony just as Samantha had visualized her wedding over the years.

The minister had just turned to her and she'd begun to say her vows when a strident voice spoke from the back.

"You slut. You've taken everything from me. You slept with him and encouraged him to not give me the position I deserved. The one I worked for." Lunette, looking distraught, held a gun pointed at Samantha's heart. Hate filled her eyes, tears ran down her face, and her appearance, usually so immaculate, was just the opposite. "I will take you from him. Just as he has taken all I wanted from me." Her hand shook, but she kept the gun aimed right at Samantha.

Shocked, the guests stared from Lunette to Samantha. Several of the men muttered and glanced at each other. Jackson stepped in front of Samantha.

"Put the gun down, Lunette. You'll have to shoot me first to get to Samantha. Let's talk. I understand—"

"You don't understand anything. I've loved you for three years. I worked hard to get your attention. While you dated stupid society women, I helped build your business. Move! Or I'll shoot you both."

Sunshine chose that moment to jump from the guest holding her and run, barking, at Lunette.

In the confusion, Drake had time to step close behind Lunette. He put his gun against her back. "Drop your gun, now." Drake's calm, cool voice warned Lunette.

She stepped forward. "I'll shoot them before you can shoot me," Lunette said. Her finger moved against the trigger. Jackson grabbed

Samantha and pushed her down, rolling so she landed on him and not the hard ground. A gunshot and then another rang out in the stunned silence.

"Are you two all right?" Samantha heard Drake call out.

Jackson sat up with Samantha in his arms. He looked at her face. "Are you?"

She nodded, unable to speak.

"Is she dead?" Jackson asked.

"No. You know I'm a better shot than that. She'll live to go to trial."

Samantha saw Drake help Lunette sit up. Blood ran down her shoulder, and her face was pale. Drake punched in numbers on his phone, probably calling the police. The guests had stood, all talking at once. Sunshine ran in circles, barking. Samantha felt both sorrow for Lunette and anger.

Jackson took charge. "The police will be here shortly. Afterwards, we'll finish our ceremony because I definitely am going to be married before we leave here." The guests gave a nervous laugh. "And after the ceremony, we'll have Maria's wonderful breakfast," he added, after the guests had settled back into their chairs.

Janice helped straighten Samantha's gown and whispered in her ear. "How do you think Drake just happened to have a gun tucked into his waistband? The man's resourceful and dangerous, like I thought from the first."

Jackson had walked to where Drake had moved Lunette. Samantha saw them step briefly to the side and talk. Then Jackson shook Drake's hand. When Jackson returned to the front, his father spoke up.

"Did he suspect trouble, or does he always carry that gun?"

"I just asked him. He said he had a bad feeling about her. Something she said to him at the barbecue, and he was there when I told her about my choice for CEO. Drake apparently decided to be on the safe side and come armed. He knew if he said anything to me, I'd have told him not to worry, that Lunette would never harm us." Jackson's face paled. "And I'd have been very wrong." He stared into Samantha's eyes. "Believe me, I'll never take a chance again with your life. The least suspicion, and I'll be prepared."

The sheriff and his deputy arrived surprisingly fast. He quickly took charge. An ambulance had followed him out. The deputy went with Lunette to the hospital. After talking with Jackson and Drake, the sheriff left with the understanding that Drake would stop by for more questioning and to sign the typed report of what he said happened today. As soon as the sheriff left, the minister took up the service from where they left off.

"I now pronounce you man and wife," the minister said. He added, "You may kiss the bride."

Jackson pulled Samantha close against him and, leaning down, kissed her. "I'll do a better job of this later," he whispered in her ear. They turned as their guests clapped their hands.

"Ladies and gentlemen, we'll meet back at the Riley ranch for that wonderful breakfast I promised," Jackson said. They stood together receiving congratulations as the people began to disperse. Some went to their trucks. Others had ridden their horses.

Samantha and Janice headed back to the tent where Samantha changed into a flowered sundress and sandals. She added a large sun hat decorated with a pink ribbon. When she came out, Jackson and Drake stood nearby.

"You two go on ahead," Drake said. "I'll wait for Janice and bring her with me."

"Thanks," Jackson said. He wrapped his arm around Samantha's waist. "I'd like a few minutes alone with my girl." Jackson led her to his black truck.

"I don't think Janice will be happy. She doesn't like Drake, or at least she says she doesn't."

"That's too bad. Drake wants her, and he usually gets what he wants."

"He might be surprised. Janice isn't your usual woman. She's not going to make it easy for him."

"I think that is part of her attraction. Now forget them." Jackson swung her around against the truck door and then leaned lightly against her. "I can't wait to have you alone tonight. We'll leave here right after breakfast in Drake's jet and will be all alone for one week." He took a nip at her earlobe.

"Still not going to tell me where we're going?"

"Nope. You'll see soon enough." He helped her get into the truck. "Let's go get this over with so we can leave."

The guests were drinking mimosas and talking amongst themselves when Samantha and Jackson arrived. Maria and her helpers soon had them all sitting at a long table set up on the porch. The roof shaded them, and a soft breeze cooled the air. Conversation flowed easily. Samantha glanced around at Gramps, Jackson's parents, and their closest friends. Except for Lunette's interruption, this had been exactly the wedding she'd wanted.

"Happy?" Jackson asked. He reached for her hand and squeezed it.

"Very. And if I drink one more of these, I'll be looped and even happier." She giggled.

"Enjoy. You can sleep on the plane. You won't get much tonight," he said and wiggled his eyebrows.

This was a beautiful moment in her life where all the pieces came together. She wished there was some way to freeze time. Samantha shivered. The thought brought back the memory of her last day with her parents. They'd gone to the beach and had cooked hot dogs over the fire as the sun went down. She remembered wishing everyday could be like that. Her father had taught her to ride the waves that day. After stuffing herself full, she'd lain back in her mother's lap, and Mama had gently caressed her forehead and hair.

Remembering her parents made her think about how horrible today could have been if Lunette hadn't been stopped. Her old fear of loss started to crowd out her happier feelings. She blinked her eyes.

"Samantha, are you all right?"

"What?" Samantha jerked herself back to the present.

"Your grandfather asked you a question, but you kept staring out in space," Jackson said. He had a worried look on his face.

"Sorry. You caught me daydreaming." She looked down the table at Gramps and saw in his face that he suspected who she'd been thinking about.

Gramps smiled. "It wasn't important. Isn't it about time for you two to leave? You have a long way to go."

"That it is, Sir." Jackson took Samantha's hand and led her around the table to tell each person good-bye. His parents kissed and hugged her.

"We're so pleased. Have a wonderful time. We'll see you when you get back," his mother said.

Last was Gramps. "I miss you already," Samantha said, low enough so only he heard.

"I'm sure Jackson will keep you busy. But, I'll be looking for you both in a week."

As they headed out, Janice ran up and gave her another hug. "Be happy."

"I will. I'll call when we get back from wherever. Jackson won't tell me our destination."

Jackson swept her into his arms and put her in his comfortable car. "We're off." He waved to the crowd, who threw birdseed at them as they drove away.

The jet had been rolled out and the engines warmed up. The pilots and one stewardess greeted them. In minutes they were in the air. When the "fasten your seat belt" light went off, Jackson took her hand. "Come. I'll show you the back of the plane."

They passed an office on the right side of the hallway, a small bath, and then Jackson opened the door at the end.

"Enter."

Samantha's feet sank into thick, dark green carpet. A large dark wood bed, with a comforter that matched the carpet and drapes, sat to the right of the door. Across from the foot of the bed was another door.

"Want to see the bathroom?" Jackson led her into a large bath of white marble. All the fixtures gleamed.

He wrapped his arms around her and pulled her close. A wicked gleam shone in his eyes. "We have a long flight ahead. Want to join the mile-high club?"

* * * *

Jackson woke Samantha just in time for her to dress and join him up front in a seat. They fastened their seat belts as the jet began its descent. Samantha leaned across Jackson to look out the window.

The beautiful sunset sent streaks of pink, purple, and gold shining over a small island. "Is that where we're headed?" She pulled back and stared at Jackson.

"Yes. Our own private getaway for the week. Actually, it's Drake's. This is his wedding present to us."

"It looks awfully small."

"It's actually a fairly large island. Wait and see, you'll like it."

The plane banked, and she got a glimpse of the runway. Samantha squeezed Jackson's hand as they landed.

When the stewardess opened the door, the scent of flowers and the sea brushed across Samantha's face. When the steps were set, Jackson stepped in front of her.

"I'll go first in case you slip. I'll be here to catch you." His smile teased. When she got to the second step from the bottom, he put his hands around her waist and swung her to the ground.

Two men walked toward them and smiled. "We are Keoni and Manu. We will drive you to the house." One of them pointed up a nearby hill.

Samantha saw a large villa built on a high level to the right of them. She followed Jackson and the men to the car. Soon they were riding along the narrow, winding road rising steadily. She glanced back just in time to see the jet take off.

"They're leaving?" Fear gripped her throat.

"They're going to another much larger island not far from here. If we need them, they can return quickly. And Keoni and Manu will be going by boat to the sister island to this one about five miles away."

He leaned closer. "Remember what I said. I'll have you all to myself."

To be honest, Samantha wasn't sure whether she was more thrilled or anxious. A whole week on a deserted island. It should be a dream come true, but she'd never been alone that long with anyone. Since she'd just recently admitted to herself that she loved Jackson, she felt more vulnerable.

"Don't look so scared, darling. I promise you'll love it."

She looked away from him, and around the curve, the house came into view. The sunset reflected in all the windows. In fact, it was almost all windows with very few walls. The car stopped at the front door, and the men took their luggage inside.

"Just leave it in the foyer," Jackson said. "We'll see you in a week. Thanks." He tipped them. They smiled and left.

Samantha heard the engine start, and the sound disappeared as they drove farther away. She turned to look at Drake's unusual home.

"Come." Jackson took her hand and led her into a room facing the west. She gasped.

The sea spread in front of them for miles. A myriad of colors cascaded across the water as the sun was setting. Up close, the land around the house gradually dropped into lower and lower terraces. Some were covered with flowering plants, and the closest held a swimming pool. Level with the house, a wide veranda invited you to step out and sit in one of the plush lawn chairs and enjoy the view.

"It's the most amazing, beautiful place I've ever seen," Samantha said, leaning back into Jackson's arms.

He nuzzled her neck. "I knew you'd love it. A great place to love and learn."

She glanced over her shoulder at him. "Love and learn?"

"Hmmm," he breathed in, his mouth against her ear. "You smell good enough to eat. But yes, learn. Even though we've known each other for years, there still must be something new to learn about each other." He stepped back. "Let's explore the house, or I could take you to bed right now?"

Samantha put her arm through his. "Let's get settled first."

Jackson smiled. "My fault. I knew better than to give you a choice."

All the rooms, except the bedrooms, opened off a large living room and all had large glass doors leading outside. The kitchen faced east. In the freezer they found frozen dinners cooked ahead for their enjoyment. In the refrigerator side, cooked shrimp, a salad, and a chilled bottle of white wine waited for them.

"Let's go for a swim, then eat," Jackson suggested.

"All right. Where is our room?"

Jackson showed her down a short hallway. There was a bedroom on each side and a door at the end of the hall. "That"—Jackson nodded to the end room—"is Drake's private retreat. We can have either of these other bedrooms. Do you want to face the sunset or sunrise?"

They walked into the room facing the sunset. The walls were a soft peach color, and the drapes and carpet were done in a deeper shade. A pretty bath adjoined, done in a light green.

"This room looks delectable. Let's stay here," she said.

I'll get the luggage." Jackson strode out and was back in a few short minutes. "Thank goodness you took me at my word and didn't pack tons of suitcases." He set the bags down and started to undress. She started to open her luggage. "Don't bother. We'll go skinny-dipping."

She stared at him. "Someone might see us. The pool is out in the open."

"Honey." Jackson stepped closer. "No one is on the island but us. We can run naked all week."

Samantha felt the heat rise to her face. "I don't think so."

"My prudish little darling. Well, I won't push you, but hopefully you'll see how relaxing it is to go without your clothes, at least some of the time. I was teasing about being naked all week." He flashed a grin. "Although it is a tantalizing thought."

She watched as he fully undressed and wrapped a towel around his middle. "I'm heading to the pool." He gave her a quick kiss and went out the door, shutting it gently behind him.

Part of her was tempted. As he said, there wasn't anyone around, and this might be the only chance she had to really loosen up. She'd try it. She took off her clothes and wrapped herself in a large beach towel she'd found in the cupboard in the bathroom. Pleasant shivers rippled down her spine as she walked toward the pool area.

* * * *

The sun had set, and Jackson put on the lights in the pool. Overhead the sky was brilliant with stars. He'd left one light on in the room beyond the veranda.

He saw her shadow first. She took his breath away as she stepped outside. The moon shone on her hair, casting a silver glow around her and the white towel she wore. She didn't say anything, but stepped close to the edge of the pool. Breathing deeply, he caught her own, personal scent.

Her hands touched in the front where the towel had been tucked in. When she opened her arms, she let the towel drop. All his blood went straight downwards. His heart pounded like a drum. The shadows cast around her hinted of lush curves. She dove into the water and came up laughing. He swam toward her. She darted in the other direction. He let her think she could get away, for a few minutes, before he sprang forward and grabbed her around the middle.

"I won." He lifted her into his arms and carried her out of the pool and across to two chairs. She slid down along his wet body as he partially released her. Grabbing the long cushions off the two chairs, he threw them onto the concrete then lowered her body to lie on them. Standing above her, he took in her beauty. "You're the best prize a man could ever receive."

Kneeling at her feet, Jackson kissed the arch of her foot and then behind her knee. Her concentrated study of his body heated his blood and urged him on. He straddled her and leaned close. "What are you thinking?"

"About how gorgeous you are naked." Her cool smile alluded to wickedness.

She touched his face. Her fingertips ran lightly over the contours of his cheeks and jaw, and along the outline of his ears. They trailed down his neck leaving a sizzling path of heat and desire.

When her hands ran through the hair of his chest and rubbed across his nipples, she stopped his breath momentarily. He didn't move. He felt too good letting her be the one in control.

Her warm hands caressed his flat abdomen, and one finger seductively circled his belly button. A shiver went up his spine as he looked into her dark, whiskey-colored eyes.

His cock had hardened and pulsed with his desire to take her, right now. When her hand circled him, he groaned.

"Like that?" Her warm-as-honey tone had him tightening his muscles to keep from burying himself in her and taking her fast and furious. He took a deep breath to control the need, the want.

She chuckled. "I like having you under my control."

"Don't be too sure of yourself," he warned.

Her hand moved up and down the length of him. She ran the fingers of her other hand gently over his sac then cupped him.

Jackson hardened even more, her touch so delicate and warm it sent a painful pleasure soaring through him. When her lips closed around him, he was certain his heart was going to leap out of his chest. She moved her mouth up and down his warm, wide cock. "You're killing me," he said with a rasp. "Enough." He startled her with his words and sudden movement. He caught the surprise in her eyes.

"You don't like this?" she asked.

"I love it. However, it's my turn." Before she said anything, he moved her onto her stomach and pulled her sweet ass up against him. "Let's try something new."

With his one hand, he touched her breast, and the other rubbed across her clit. "Relax, darling, trust me, you'll like this." Her gorgeous hair hid her face, but she wiggled against his tight belly

He couldn't wait. Desire throbbed through his every cell. He moved his cock in place, and in one smooth glide, he entered her from behind. Her hot, tight pussy clamped around him, sending an electric jolt sizzling along his nerves.

His fingers rubbed across her clit, and she moved that sweet ass hard against him. He started the rhythm, in and out. Heat pulsed around him and in him. Her moan almost made him lose it, but he waited until he felt her contractions start and then buried himself deep and hard as they both came together.

Heart pounding, he rolled to the side. When he could breathe normally, he brushed her hair back. She'd cuddled close to him. "All right?"

"If I was any better, I'd explode into tiny stars and float up into the sky."

A tiny worry tried to enter his mind. He pushed it away. He'd deal with problems as they came. She was finally his, and he'd never lose her. Whatever it took.

* * * *

Samantha lay beside Jackson, listening to his breathing. Her body still tingled from their lovemaking. Now that she had admitted she loved him, their coming together was even sweeter. She reached out and ran her hand over his hard body. He gently took hold of her wrist.

"This time it's my turn." He brushed her hair away from her face and neck then nipped at the lobe of her ear with his teeth. "You are a delectable buffet, my dear." He wiggled his eyebrows, making her laugh. When he came to the sweet spot between shoulder and neck, he found her ticklish spot. She giggled and tried to move away, but he had her at his mercy. He teased with her, and gradually the playfulness began to warm her body in a different way.

His mouth kissed her mound then he separated her lower lips and tasted her. His tongue slid seductively across her clit. Her lower body rose to seek more of his attention.

This time their lovemaking was slower, like a sultry dance. Instead of fire, warm honey ran through her veins, and when he slowly entered, moving inch by inch along her hot pussy, desire swirled so intensely she'd swear she tasted the sweetness. Her climax came softly, enveloping her body in a cloud of warmth and love.

Later they cuddled on a soft rug in front of the fireplace. The only light inside the house came from the flames. Outside, the stars twinkled and the moon sent silver shining across the polished wood floor. Samantha had never been happier or more content. Most of her life she'd been frightened of being too happy. She pushed away the brief flash of fear that coursed through her, reminding her of the danger of being vulnerable.

As though he'd felt her internal shiver, Jackson pulled her closer, kissed the top of her head, and whispered in her ear, *"I'm here, love, always."* But was it a promise he could keep?

Chapter Ten

The next few days were like a wonderful dream. They swam in the warm waters of the ocean and walked along the sand finding beautiful sea shells. Samantha gathered the prettiest to keep and take home as a souvenir of their honeymoon.

On Wednesday, when she awoke, Jackson had already left their bed. She found him in the kitchen making peanut butter and jelly sandwiches.

"Is that our breakfast?" she asked.

"Our lunch. I've set juice and fruit on a tray in the refrigerator. Pour our coffee and take the tray out to the table on the veranda." He nodded his head toward the glass doors. "I'll bring the coffee in a minute. I'm almost finished here."

Samantha took their breakfast tray outside. She sipped her orange juice and admired the lush scenery in front of her. Bees buzzed around the flowers. The sky was an intense blue with a few wispy clouds floating lazily along on the sea breeze.

"Here's your coffee." Jackson handed her a cup. He sat down beside her. "Between you and this view, I could sit here all day and just soak in the beauty."

"Flattery will get you somewhere," she teased.

"Do you feel up to exploring the north end of the island today? We'll have to walk several miles, some of it uphill."

"Sounds good to me. We've been eating such rich meals, steak, lobster, shrimp, not to mention the wonderful desserts. I can use the exercise."

"I thought I'd been giving you plenty of that."

Samantha gave him a wry smile. "Right, but that doesn't burn off enough calories."

"I can try harder."

She laughed. "You're insatiable."

"With you, I am. But, you're right. We need the exercise. It'll be fun. Drake and I walked around the area the last time I visited. He showed me a really nice spot that's perfect for a picnic."

After finishing her coffee, Samantha stretched. "I'll wear jeans and a shirt with my bathing suit underneath just in case we find a place to swim."

"Or you could wear nothing underneath."

"You are incorrigible." She waved and headed inside.

Shortly afterwards, they started their walk. First, a gentle slope that leveled off for some distance, and then they began to climb. Samantha felt the strain on leg muscles she didn't usually use.

"Tired?" Jackson asked. "We can stop here to rest."

"Let's. I want to drink some water. It's hotter today."

She took a bottle out of her knapsack and found a shady spot to sit. Here the trees grew closer together. Sunlight barely found a place to peek through the thick branches. She took off her hat and wet the scarf, holding her hair back, with the water from her thermos, and then wiped her face before taking a deep swallow from the bottle.

Jackson swung down beside her. He'd also gotten water out of his knapsack. "Look over there." He pointed to a cluster of trees to their right. "See the orchids growing wild?" The small cluster of white blooms, with purple trim, moved gently in the breeze.

Samantha leaned her head against the massive tree trunk behind her. "I don't see how Drake can manage to leave this place."

"It's his getaway. He escapes here when the work gets too intense. But, he loves the excitement of his job too much to stay for long."

She turned her head to look at Jackson. "Aren't you going to miss the fast pace of traveling, making big deals, going to parties? Are you sure the ranch won't bore you after a time?"

He tipped her chin up and gave her a quick kiss. "It wasn't a quick decision. I took my time and thought about all the pros and cons over many months."

"What decided you in the end?"

"I missed the slower pace of the ranch and the way I felt when I was there. Plus, the people are so genuine." He hesitated then added, "I'd pretty much explored what I needed to do to make the change and had begun to implement my plan." He pulled her close against his side. "When you proposed, that really sealed the deal."

Jackson stood and pulled her up. "Let's go. Not too much farther. If you like this spot, you'll love where we picnic."

He put his knapsack on his back and helped her with hers.

About a half hour later, they arrived at the top. Thick trees made a ring around a small lake. Sunlight sparked off the water, and at the other end, a waterfall cascaded down the mountain.

"The water's cold, but refreshing," Jackson said. "Before we get wet, walk with me between these trees."

Outside the trees, the view of a glorious span of white sand and crystal-clear blue water spread out for miles before them. Jackson stepped behind her and wrapped his arms around her.

"At the top of the world, just me and my girl." He kissed the side of her face. "Just think, we have all our lives to enjoy each other and all the children we hope to have."

"Don't say things like that out loud," Samantha cautioned.

"Why not?" Jackson turned her to face him. "Don't tell me you're superstitious?"

Samantha hugged him tight. "I'm afraid to be *too* happy."

Jackson kissed the top of her head. "Just living has risks. I promise I'll be there for both the ups and downs."

She shivered. "What if you die?"

He leaned back and cupped her face. "There are no guarantees, sweetheart. You could have been shot on our wedding day. All I can promise is today." He stared directly into her eyes. "Losing your parents at an early age was very hard, and you didn't expect your grandmother's death. You loved them. Loving is risky." He put his arm around her. "Come on. Let's enjoy our picnic. Enough serious talk for now."

Stepping around him, she went back through the trees to the lake. She watched as Jackson cut an orchid and brought it to her. He tucked it behind her ear.

"My island princess."

After spreading a blanket, they set out the peanut butter sandwiches, bananas, and leftover barbecue chicken from the night before. They ate quietly, listened to the music of the water falling, the rustle of leaves, and enjoyed the relaxing view while sipping from the bottle of champagne Jackson had brought. He'd stuck the bottle in the cold water to chill it. After they finished, Samantha repacked the leftover food into their knapsack. She walked to the edge of the small lake and tested the temperature with her foot.

"It's cold."

"Drake said the water comes from a natural spring, and this area is shaded, which helps to keep it cold. Want to swim?"

"Maybe another day. I'm too comfortable to plunge into cold water." She mimicked a mock shiver.

"I'd warm you when you came out."

She stepped to the edge of the blanket. "You can warm me, but I'll skip the swim." She slowly began to disrobe, dropping her blouse, and then very slowly, she unzipped her jeans and pushed them down and off. Her bikini top followed.

Jackson took her hand and pulled her down beside him. "I'll take care of the rest." He rolled to his side and touched the side of her face. Leaning toward her, he kissed the top of her nose. "I love these freckles you've gotten from the sun." He ran his tongue over her lips. "I always think of raspberry jam when I kiss you." Moving along, he let out a long breath against her skin before he kissed her neck. "Your scent reminds me of old roses in the summer, the most fragrant kind."

Her heart beat faster as he slid down each part of her body, tasting and touching. His hand caressed her legs, and then he opened them, moving his kisses to her tender lower lips. His tongue licked and swirled over her.

He glanced up at her and smiled before putting his hard cock against her pussy and smoothly gliding in as far as possible.

She melted totally. His lovemaking wove a spell as he continued to take his time bringing her almost to the edge and pulling back.

She raised her hips, urging him, wanting him to move faster and harder. He held back, until the very end when he surged forward fast, hard, and deep. He captured her mouth as she yelled, "Yes!"

They lay side by side, letting their breathing return to normal. The shade cooled their hot bodies. When Jackson's breathing had slowed, he swung one leg over her and held her face so she looked right at him.

"Loving you one day, two years, or forever, I'll take whatever time I get."

His eyes shone a deep blue sapphire color. Her fingers brushed across his well-formed mouth. His lips opened, and he took a nip at her fingertip.

"I hate to end this," he said. "But, if we don't start back, we'll run out of daylight before we get to the house."

They dressed and put their knapsacks on their shoulders.

Samantha took a last glance over her shoulder.

"We'll come back," Jackson reassured her. "We have a few more days left."

At first her legs were weak from their previous exertion. When they reached the flatter area, the walk got easier. Gradually, the mansion in the sky, as she liked to think of it, came into sight, which encouraged them to move more rapidly.

"Why does it always seem to take less time when you're going back from somewhere?" Samantha asked as they stepped onto the veranda.

"I don't know, but it does appear that way. I'll check my phone. Too bad we can't take it on our outings. This is one of the few areas that has good coverage."

Samantha headed straight for the bathroom, quickly shed her clothes, and jumped into the shower. She'd washed her hair and was almost finished with her bath when Jackson came into the room. She knew when she saw his face that something bad had happened.

Turning off the faucet, she grabbed her towel and stepped out. "What is it?"

"We need to get home. Your grandfather has taken ill and is in the hospital. I've called for the jet."

"Gramps? What's the matter with him?" Her heart sank, and all her old fears came back.

Jackson pulled her to him and hugged her. "I brought the phone. Here, call Maria. See if she's at the house."

Her fingers shook so bad Jackson took the phone and put in the numbers for her. She took it back and listened as it rang and rang.

"Who did you talk to?" she asked Jackson.

"No one. Maria left a very brief message. Let's pack. I've called for the jet. It'll be here soon."

She threw her clothes into the suitcase and went around the house with Jackson, making sure all was locked and shut off before they left. They had just finished in the kitchen when Samantha spotted the plane in the distance. "They're almost here."

She ran to get her suitcase, and Jackson wasn't far behind her.

Keoni and Manu had been notified and arrived in time to hurriedly drive them to the landing strip. Her heart pounded as the jet took off. *Hurry, hurry, I can't get there too late. I have to see Gramps.*

Jackson took her hand in his. He raised it to his lips and kissed her knuckles.

"A car will be waiting in Houston. We'll be able to get right to the hospital."

Samantha hardly heard his words. She saw the last of the sunset sink into the west, and the shadows of fear sank into her. This was one time going back took forever. She slept in snatches during the flight.

Fear gripped her throat tight again after they landed. The limousine sped around traffic to get them to the hospital. Jackson held her arm as they walked along the hospital corridor to the cardiac ICU waiting room.

All medical centers had a familiar smell—a combination of cleaning agents, perfumed air, and people. Samantha twitched her nose. Hospitals were not her favorite places, especially not waiting rooms. They were bare and cold, usually had no windows, or if the room had one, there was no view, except another building. The particular scent smelled of anxiety and a cross between fear and hope.

As soon as she saw Samantha, Maria ran into her arms. "I'm so sorry you had to cut your trip short. Mr. Riley said not to call, but I knew you'd want to know."

"Absolutely, you did the right thing," Samantha reassured her.

"Sit, then tell me what happened and why he had surgery." She directed Maria to a chair and sat beside her.

"He's been having trouble with his heart," Maria said. She raised her hand before Samantha could ask a question. "He swore me to secrecy. Said he didn't want to put a damper on your wedding plans. He wanted to be there to see you wed."

"Is that why he made those unannounced visits to Saddle Creek and then to Houston?" Samantha asked.

"Yes. The doctors in both places told him he needed bypass surgery, but he put it off. He planned to have it later after you came back." Tears ran down Maria's face. "The stubborn man. His heart didn't wait. He had a heart attack. The doctors said it was a mild one, thankfully. They took him right to surgery." Maria wiped her eyes and gave a weak laugh. "I'm sure he was arguing with the doctors right up to when they put him to sleep."

"That sounds like Gramps. How long will they be keeping him in

ICU?" Samantha asked.

Maria smiled. "His doctor said maybe tomorrow he'd go to the cardiac floor."

"That's good news," Jackson said. "I'm going to find us all a cup of coffee and maybe some food." He kissed Samantha. "I won't be long."

"You're happy?" Maria asked after he left.

"Very, but I'm really concerned about Gramps. I was so frightened during the flight here."

"The doctors are very encouraged, and now that you've arrived, I'm sure he'll do even better." Maria patted her back. "It's all going to be good from now on."

* * * *

Two days later, standing outside Gramps' hospital door, Samantha remembered Maria's prediction. Jackson had supposedly left early to go by his old business, so she'd decided to surprise Gramps at breakfast. But, she got the surprise. She'd started to push the door open when she heard Gramps' voice and then Jackson's. Apparently, they'd been talking for some time.

"This wasn't our agreement," Gramps said. "The will has been written so you get fifty-one percent of the Riley ranch when I die. You're to name the first son Riley, and eventually it'll all go to him. That's a good deal. No more discussion. Don't you have somewhere to go?"

Jackson laughed. "You're a cantankerous old man. I'll agree for now."

Shocked, Samantha hurried away from the door. She went around the opposite corner from the elevators. Jackson strode out of Gramps' room, and the elevator door opened just as he approached. She waited until the door closed then sank against the wall. Hot tears rolled down her cheeks.

No wonder he'd wanted to marry soon before Gramps changed his mind. Had that been his payoff to marry her? He got the majority share of her ranch, meaning whatever she suggested he could say no to. Angrily, she wiped the tears from her face. They'd both betrayed her. The two men she'd trusted the most. Her heart ached with the pain of betrayal. Glancing around, she saw the sign for the stairwell.

She took the stairs and came out in the back of the hospital. Since she'd taken a taxi, she didn't have to worry about her car. Where to go? She wandered along the busy streets, not noticing what direction she'd taken. When she got thirsty, she stopped at an outdoor cafe and ordered tea and toast. She didn't think anything else would stay down. All around her, people hurried on foot and in cars. They had places to go, people to see. There wasn't anyone for her to talk with except Janice.

Samantha took out her cell phone and punched in the number. Janice came right to the phone.

"Sam, where are you? Jackson called, frantic. He said Mrs. Murphy told him you'd left early for the hospital, but you never arrived."

"I arrived just in time to overhear Gramps and Jackson's conversation." Samantha started to cry. "He married me for the ranch. In fact, Gramps bought me a husband."

"You're talking crazy. Tell me where you are, and I'll come and get you."

"If I do, you mustn't let anyone else know."

"Jackson's worried, Sam. Your grandfather will be, too, if you don't get over to the hospital. Sam?"

Thoughts went round and round in her head. She didn't want Gramps to have a relapse. "Meet me across the street from the hospital at the coffee shop. We'll talk. You can tell them I'm all right, and I'll be along later. Don't say where you're meeting me."

"I don't like it, but all right." Janice rang off.

Samantha backtracked. The next few hours were going to be the hardest when she confronted Jackson. She'd been so sure he loved her. But, he couldn't. Not to have agreed to being given controlling interest in the Riley ranch. He had to know how hurt she'd be. She understood Gramps. He wanted to see her safe and wed.

Janice parked at the curb just as Samantha had found a quiet table in the back of the shop. Samantha noted the worried expression on her friend's face. Spotting her, Janice walked around the mostly empty tables and dropped into the seat across from her.

"Have you lost your mind?" Janice asked. "Jackson adores you. And he's rich. He doesn't need the ranch."

"You're wrong."

"No, you are. You may be my best friend, but right now I'm really angry with you. Talk to Jackson, hear his side."

"I hurt so bad. Ever since I heard them talking."

"Did you listen to the whole conversation?"

"I arrived toward the end. It doesn't matter. I heard enough."

Janice groaned and shook her head. "Did you have a good time on your trip?"

"Yes."

"And Jackson was attentive and loving?"

"Of course, it was a honeymoon."

"Well, if you're right then he didn't have to be. He had what you say he wanted as soon as you became his wife."

"Not really. He has to stay around until Gramps dies."

"Listen to yourself. You've known Jackson for years. Do you really think he's capable of such devious behavior?"

Samantha's hot tea began to warm the cold spot inside her. She thought about what Janice said. Truly, the Jackson she thought she knew would never even consider being devious or deliberately hurting anyone. She remembered what Mr. Greenlee and his wife had said about him.

Janice reached out and touched her hand. "Talk to him. I'll call and ask him to come here."

"Thank you. I don't know why I reacted so strongly. The news shook me. Why did Gramps do it, if not to get me a husband?"

"Think about how your Gramps sees the world. I've got to go back to work. Call me later."

"I will."

The waitress brought her a fresh pot of hot water and another tea bag. She heard each long minute as the hand of the old clock scraped across the surface. Traffic buzzed by. She'd looked down to add sugar to her tea when she sensed him there.

He stood inside the door staring at her, his eyes dark as night and his face pale. Slowly, he walked to her table and sat.

"You gave me a scare." The words came out flat and hard. All the planes of his face were etched with worry and, underneath, anger. The anger, a pulsing entity around them.

She didn't know what to say to him.

"I saw my attorney. You can have a divorce. If I haven't been able to convince you of my love by now, nothing will."

He scraped his chair back and stood. His hand reached into his suit jacket and pulled an envelope out. He laid it in front of her.

"I had this drawn up before our wedding. Your grandfather wouldn't let me tell you about his will. I begged him not to do what he did. He's an obstinate old man." A half smile curved his mouth. "He swore me to secrecy. I knew this day would come, sooner or later. I'd hoped later. I believed, no, hoped, you'd come to me at the time, talk with me, give me a chance." His shoulders slumped as he turned and slowly walked off.

What have I done? Samantha's hand touched the envelope. Part of her was afraid to read what lay inside. She pulled out the paper and unfolded it. At first, the dark letters blurred. She blinked, and as her vision cleared, she read the short, official contract.

He'd signed fifty-one percent of his ranch over to her a few days before their wedding. Her heart sank. She'd been stupid and overreacted. In the end, she'd allowed her fears to help her lose the best thing she'd ever had, Jackson's love.

Chapter Eleven

Samantha kissed Gramps' cheek. "I'm going for a ride. Do you need anything before I go?"

"No. Stay outside awhile. You look pale, worse than me." He smiled and patted her hand. "You're sure Jackson doesn't mind you staying here? After all, you two are newlyweds, and I already interrupted your honeymoon."

"He's fine with it," Samantha lied again. She was becoming good at telling false tales. She hadn't seen Jackson since the day at the coffee shop. She'd heard he visited Gramps at the hospital, but never when she was there.

She'd made up the story of them deciding for her to stay at Gramps' and help Maria until he was able to get out and about. Her days consisted of seeing he got his walks and that he wasn't lonely. Once a day, she went out for a ride. Every day she had to fight the temptation to ride to Jackson's. She would if he was there, and she knew what to say. As far as she knew, he had stayed in Houston.

She saddled her mare, Princess, and headed out. Overhead, the sky had a rich blue color that reminded her of Jackson. A few wisps of clouds slowly moved across, and a slight breeze ruffled the leaves in the oak trees. She kidded herself that she let the mare lead the way, but every day she ended in the same place—her outdoor cathedral where they had wed.

Samantha dismounted and tied Princess close to the small stream where she could drink. Nothing around her had changed since they'd had their wedding here. Everything had changed for her, and not the way she'd expected or hoped. Of course, the chairs and decorations were long gone, and the days were hot now. Here, the shade and water kept the area a bit cooler. She sank onto the ground beneath the trees and cried. She'd held in the grief around Gramps and Maria. Only here could she release the pent-up pain.

After her cry, she leaned her head back and stared through the tree branches to the sky. This wasn't like her at all. She went after what she wanted. Sitting here feeling sorry for herself accomplished nothing. She'd created the problem. She'd fix it.

She straightened her shoulders. She knew what to do. She might fail—no, she refused to consider any result but success.

Eager to put her idea to action, Samantha mounted Princess and rode quickly back to the ranch. Gramps was much better. He'd be pleased to think she was going to spend a few days with her husband. By afternoon, she'd be on her way to Houston.

* * * *

Jackson paced around his townhouse. He'd helped Greenlee as much as the man wanted. He knew his new CEO was ready to do his job on his own. For Jackson to stay here any longer would give the impression he didn't trust the choice he'd made. Sooner or later he had to return to the ranch. He'd been so anxious to do that just a few weeks ago. Without Samantha, though, the idea wasn't as pleasing.

He loved ranching, so he'd just bury himself in the work. If only she'd tried to contact him. Still, he hadn't received any divorce papers, which was the only thing that gave him hope.

He'd phone Mrs. Haverty and tell Anna, who was in the kitchen cleaning, to plan on moving to the ranch anytime in the next few weeks. There were several available homes on the ranch, and they'd each chosen one to live in.

But first, he'd call Fred, his pilot. He answered on the second ring. "Have the helicopter ready to take off tomorrow morning, early," Jackson said.

"Yes, Sir. Is seven a good time?

"Fine. I'll meet you at the airport." Jackson put down the phone. He'd leave tonight, but he'd accepted an invitation to a cocktail party at Mr. Greenlee's home. He'd surprise his new CEO and let him know he was finally leaving him on his own.

His mood wasn't the best for a party. He didn't plan on staying long. Since the day he'd last seen Samantha and handed her that envelope, his heart had been heavy with pain. Aloneness had never bothered him before, but now he had to stay busy or go crazy wandering around the rooms in his townhouse. He hadn't had one good night of sleep, and he knew it was beginning to show. Hurt and anger still warred inside him. He had difficulty believing how quickly she'd thought the worst of him. So many times he'd been tempted to fly to the ranch, demand to see her, and take her home to his ranch. He'd make love to her, talk to her, not let her go until she knew how wrong she'd been.

In the end, he'd always worry what would happen the next time she thought she had a reason to doubt him. So, he waited, *for her*, and he'd not heard a word.

Reluctantly, he went to his bedroom to pack and change for the party. In here he had the most difficult time keeping her out of his thoughts. Everywhere he looked, he saw her, remembered the softness of her skin, the taste of her. Her particular special scent lingered in his mind. *Damn, get dressed and get out of here.*

Tomorrow, he'd start fresh. But, she'd still follow him. There were even more poignant memories all around him at his ranch.

* * * *

Samantha had made two phone calls before she left. One to Janice to arrange for a place to stay for the night, in case she needed one. The other call was to the office. Mr. Greenlee told her Jackson had not been in but was expected at the cocktail party he and his wife were giving. Of course, he'd invited her.

The pieces were falling into place for her plan to begin. Her heart beat rapidly. This had to work. She went directly to Janice's when she arrived. The drive to Houston had given her plenty of time to think.

Janice had arrived home just before Samantha got there. "I'm glad you've finally come to your senses."

Samantha put down her luggage. "I came to them the day he met me at the coffee shop. I just didn't know what to do about the situation."

"Are you going to call him or what?"

"I'm going to a cocktail party. I've been assured he'll be there."

She'd brought the dress she'd worn to the other party, the bronze-colored cocktail dress. When she put it on, Janice laughed. "You know, I almost feel sorry for him. He hasn't a chance when he sees you in that outfit."

Samantha added the oval diamond necklace and matching earrings. She spun around. "How do I look?"

"All the wives will hate you. No one wants such a stunning woman anywhere near their husbands."

"Too much?"

"Oh, no. Just what you need to catch and hold his attention."

"He might give me the cold shoulder."

Janice laughed. "If he stares blankly, it's only because all his blood has gone straight to his cock."

"Janice!"

"Crude, but honest. Go get him." Janice urged her forward. "You know where the Greenlees live?"

"Mr. Greenlee gave me instructions. Funny, he didn't seem surprised I wasn't coming with Jackson."

"I'm sure all the staff is aware something happened. I ran into Jackson earlier in the week. He looked awful. I started to call you, but thought better of it. You two have to fix this yourselves."

Samantha hugged Janice. "You are so wise. How is your love life doing?"

"I don't have one."

"You haven't heard from Drake?"

"Oh, him? He's pestered me a few times."

"He won't give up trying."

"I won't give up saying no," Janice said.

"Silly girl." Samantha waved on her way out the door. When she got into the car, she sat a minute. A wave of nausea came over her. Nerves. She took a deep breath before starting the car. Her heart pounded. Her future hung on how she handled this evening.

* * * *

Jackson recognized her the minute he stepped inside the Greenlees' large living room. Her golden hair brushed across the bare skin of her back and that sweet ass sent his heart rate straight up and his blood straight down.

What was she doing here? He was afraid to hope he might be the reason. Then she turned and smiled.

He'd seen that open, joyous smile the first time years ago. They'd been riding around the two ranches and stopped in a wide open pasture. She dismounted and stood among the bluebells blooming across the land for as far as they could see. In the wind, the flowers rippled like waves on the ocean. The sunlight and the bright blue of the sky were almost blinding.

She'd thrown her arms open to hug the world.

"Isn't this the most beautiful day you've ever seen?"

It was, and she was part of that gorgeous scene forever etched in his memory. Now, she started slowly walking toward him. He barely took a breath while watching her. Hope began to fill his heart. She stopped close, staring directly into his eyes.

"I'm sorry. Can you forgive me? I know it will take time for you to ever trust me, but I promise I won't doubt you or your integrity ever again. My foolish fears of losing love may have cost me a love I can't replace. I've missed you." The words rushed out of her.

He forgot all the people around them and pulled her into his arms. "I've been miserable without you. Let's go home."

She hugged him tight then looked up at him. "Home here or the ranch?"

"The ranch. My real home is anywhere you are." Jackson glanced around and noticed the guests had quietly moved into the adjoining family room, leaving them to their privacy.

He cradled her head. "I'll never let you go if you leave with me now," he said and scattered kisses over her face.

Samantha stood on her tiptoes, her arms around his neck, and she looked him right in the eye. "Good." She kissed him while she let her soft, curvy body sink into him.

Moving her attention to his ear, she nibbled on his earlobe. "We'd better leave before we embarrass the Greenlees and their guests."

Jackson hurried them through their good-byes and soon had them headed to the townhouse. "I've already ordered the 'copter to take me to the ranch early tomorrow, never expecting I'd have you with me."

"I drove."

"I'll take care of having someone bring the car to us. You're not getting out of my sight anytime soon. I have plans to keep you very busy."

She laughed and hugged his arm as they sped through the dark streets. "I do hope those plans include lots of loving."

They'd stopped at a light. He looked at her. Streetlights reflected across her beautiful eyes, her sweet mouth curved into a tempting smile, and her lovely luscious body called to him on some unseen level. His cock went so hard it hurt. "You aren't going to get much sleep, my love."

"Promises, promises." Her laughter rang out like music to his starved soul.

Epilogue

One Year Later

Jackson and Samantha walked into Gramps' house. She deliberately let the door slam.

"I always know when you arrive, Samantha." Gramps gave a fake grumble from where he stood in the doorway to his study. "I thought you'd never get here."

Sunshine came running from the kitchen. She excitedly barked and jumped against Samantha's legs. Samantha leaned down to rub her fur.

"I think you just gave me that dog to annoy me," Gramps said, but he had a twinkle in his eye. "And if Maria keeps feeding her, she'll be nothing but a round ball of fur."

"There you are." Maria came out of the kitchen drying her hands on a towel. "And you've brought the little one."

"I get to hold him first," Gramps said.

Samantha walked across to Gramps and settled his namesake, Colin Riley Stone, in his arms. She enjoyed seeing the glow on Gramps' face every time he saw or held his great-grandchild. His health had improved immensely since his bypass operation.

"You two gave me my wish. I asked for a great-grandchild, and you gave me one. I think you'll have to have another one, though, preferably a girl, and then Maria will have a baby to hold, too." He winked his eye at Maria and smiled at Samantha and Jackson. "You've made this old man very happy."

Jackson put his arm around Samantha and pulled her close. "It was really no effort at all, Sir. We'll get started right away on your new request." They all laughed when Samantha blushed.

She gazed around the room at all her loved ones. Her son slept comfortably in Gramps' arms. He was a mixture of Jackson and her, having her blonde hair and Jackson's eye color.

Occasionally, Samantha's fear of loss tried to come back. Especially on nights when Jackson and the baby were close by her side. They were all safe and secure inside their home. Her happiness, in those moments, swelled over her like a wave filling her heart and bringing with it just a touch of fear. Jackson always sensed her uneasiness and quickly reassured her. Usually by first talking and teasing her, and then followed with a hot session of sex. That always worked.

Samantha had cuddled against Jackson's shoulder. She tipped her head up at him. His eyes sparkled with mischief and that tantalizing hint of lust. His lips brushed across her mouth.

"We'd better leave if we want to get to Houston before noon," Jackson said.

"You're sure you guys will be all right for a few hours with Colin?" Samantha asked.

Maria looked at her sternly. "What a question. Of course."

Samantha smiled. "Just checking."

"Great." Jackson started edging her toward the door.

"Have fun on your birthday, Samantha," Gramps said.

"We brought formula, clothes, and everything we could think of that you might need. If a question comes up, call the ranch. The nanny is taking the morning off, but she'll be near the phone, and she'll pick him up around one. We won't be back until later this evening."

Jackson pulled her arm. "Come on."

Reluctantly, she let him lead her to the truck. She waved and looked back until Maria, Gramps, and Colin were out of sight. "He will be all right?"

"Of course. We've left him with them before."

"But not when we were going to be so far away."

"They'll do fine, and if needed, there's plenty of help nearby. Relax, it's your day."

The 'copter ride went quickly. They soon landed on the roof of the townhouse. Jackson helped her out and then carried the small case they'd brought with them down the stairs.

They stepped inside the closed-up apartment. Samantha turned on the air while Jackson put the bag down inside the master suite. "At last." Jackson lowered his head and kissed her. "We can change and go shopping for your birthday present—or—we can enjoy our alone time first." He smiled, making her heart beat faster. "My vote is for the alone time." His husky tone sent shivers down her spine.

Samantha gave the appearance of giving his idea much thought. She tipped her head and put one finger to her lip. "Hmmm, a difficult decision." She wrinkled her forehead and then began to very slowly unbutton her blouse.

"I'll beat you to the shower." She laughed and ran toward the decadent bathroom.

Jackson caught her and swung her into his arms. "I won."

He let her down so that her body slid along his. "Let me help you." He reached for her blouse to finish unbuttoning it.

Her hands went right to his belt buckle, and in seconds, she had her fingers wrapped around his hard, hot cock. She knelt in front of him and ran her tongue along the ridged top. She licked off the salty drop that had seeped out.

He'd let go of her blouse, and now his hands ran through her hair. "This is your birthday, and I'm getting the present." He gasped as she took him in further, her tongue touching and tasting. She cupped his sac as she tightened her lips on his cock. His hands clenched tighter in her hair.

"Stop, I'm going to lose it. I want to come in you."

He raised her up to face him. "Hell with the shower. Come here."

Taking her hand, he guided her to the stool in front of the dressing table. He sat and had her straddle her legs on either side of him.

She guided his cock to her pussy, and Jackson pulled her down. His thick cock went deep. She moved, taking him in even further. His hands cupped her breasts as his mouth found hers.

He filled her and surrounded her. She clenched and unclenched her inner muscles, sending hot pleasure flowing through her veins.

Jackson began to move her up and down. When he raised her, he suckled on her breasts, and then he lowered her and nibbled on her neck. She ached and throbbed for him. "More, more," she whispered.

Standing, he carried her to the wall, holding her legs around him. Now he surged in and out faster and harder. Her arms tightened around his neck. She matched his rhythm. Her inside muscles clamped around his cock began to quiver, and then a mixture of heat, an ache, and almost unbearable pleasure had her closing down on him hard and hollering his name. His hot seed filled her almost instantly.

Jackson leaned his head on the wall above her. "Woman, you'll be the death of me."

Both their hearts pounded against each other. She laughed. "And you me."

He lowered her feet to the floor. "I did promise Gramps a great-granddaughter," Jackson said. "We may have succeeded already."

"I'm certain we'll have to work on it some more," Samantha purred into his ear.

Jackson hugged her. "If you insist. First, though, I need to get a present for my wife's birthday."

"Do you think she expects a gift?"

"I'm sure." He kissed her mouth. "She's a very demanding woman."

Laughing, Samantha stepped into the shower. Jackson started to follow her. She stopped him. "If you get in, we'll be late for our lunch engagement."

"The hell with them. It's only our two best friends. Let me in there, woman."

Samantha opened the shower door and her arms. "Your command is my wish, love."

He moved her hair aside and kissed the spot between her neck and shoulder. "This is your birthday, and I intend to take every advantage I can." Warm water pulsated over them as their bodies came together.

"Our friends will never forgive us if we don't show up," she whispered in his ear.

"Yes, they will," he whispered back. "I lied about the lunch so we'd have more time alone. Mrs. Haverty called early this morning and rearranged our lunch to dinnertime."

She laughed as clouds of heat began to surround them, and not just from the water.

THE END

WWW.PAIGECAMERON.COM

ABOUT THE AUTHOR

Born in Florida, Paige Cameron's early dreams included being a movie star. Of course, it didn't happen. Later, she escaped into daydreams full of fascinating stories. Her friends had to endure her reading those tales to them when she began to put them to paper.

There were detours in her life for marriage, children, traveling to foreign countries where her husband's job took her. She continued to be an avid reader and dream of the day she'd have a book published. She finally got started writing and divorce side tracked her.

Now, happily married to her hero, with grown children, she decided to pursue her dream career, writing.

Also by Paige Cameron

Siren Classic: *The Earl's Intriguing Imposter*
Siren Classic: *Scandalous Seduction*
Everlasting Classic: *The Duke's Blind Temptation*
Everlasting Classic: *Propositioned by a Lady*

Available at
BOOKSTRAND.COM

Siren Publishing, Inc.
www.SirenPublishing.com

CPSIA information can be obtained at www.ICGtesting.com
Printed in the USA
238370LV00009B/54/P